"Minnow" Vail

"Minnow" Vail

By WINIFRED E. WISE

cover and decorations by
MIMI KORACH

A WHITMAN BOOK
Western Publishing Company, Inc., Racine, Wisconsin

Produced in U.S.A.

Library of Congress Catalog Card Number: 62-15254

Contents

1

Wild Moods

One of the great advantages of beachcombing, thought Minna Vail fervently, was the fact that you were a million miles away from people—particularly people like Mrs. Latham who had the nerve to call you on the telephone and ask you to be a Grunion. Imagine being a Grunion at the Carnival again this year, when you were actually going on sixteen!

Justified resentment surged within her. She had come running down to the shore, always her refuge, as soon as she had hung up the phone. A Grunion! It was actually almost an insult! She was obviously Mermaid material; anybody should be able to see that! Last year was all right; she hadn't minded being grouped with the rest of the beach city's small fry. But everything was different now. At least it ought to be!

Striding along the deserted stretch of beach in the

late February afternoon, alone in her favorite place of all places, Minna found herself relaxing. It was hard to do justice to her grievance; the muffled roaring of the mighty Pacific acted almost as a tranquilizer and a stimulant all in one. The bigness of it made her problems seem smaller in spite of herself. " 'There are many seas, but here is the one ocean, and here the heavy future hangs like a cloud . . .' " as her father was fond of quoting to her.

The tide was out, way, way out, uncovering much of the sea floor. The rippled sands were strewn with what might just possibly prove to be treasures. The winter storms could bring almost anything to shore—shells seldom found along this particular coast, or a rare variety of starfish, or wave-smoothed driftwood or even the wreckage of what might once have been a fair ship. " 'Oh, I have a fair ship on the ocean, all covered with silver and gold. . . .' " That was one of her father's songs.

It was hard, almost impossible, to stay angry now. The sea, her own sea, had cleaned house as it often did in the roistering winter, and Minna never knew when she went down to the shore what booty she might stumble upon. That was the thrill of it in these precious hours away from high school and away from home, poking in the glistening piles of kelp uprooted by rough water from the ocean's depths and racy with its clean breath. Today she found herself a rescuer of little crabs left stranded by the tide. The poor things had a right to stay alive; everything did. Except maybe mosquitos and snakes, neither of which frequented Cliffside.

Minna put all her grievances in the back of her mind, and let the spell of the seashore take her. She often felt herself a daughter of the sea, a water sprite, an Undine. It was not only because of her small stature that everyone called her "Minnow." When it could be managed at all, she was usually beside the ocean or in it. Now, as a larger wave came rolling in and suddenly swept to the knees of her jeans, she stooped to feel its chill against her wrists, to scoop up foam and fling it high. There was nobody around to spoil the moment. The beach was deserted as usual with the near approach of twilight; the entire strand, beginning to reflect the soft colors of sunset, belonged only to Minna and the sea birds, the circling gulls and the tiny sandpipers that skittered along like toys on wheels. Fashioning a jump rope of kelp, she skipped happily after them, unashamed. If any of her classmates had chanced to see her, she would never have heard the end of it. "That Minnow Vail is a real-gone nut!" they would say. Not that she cared, really.

Perhaps she was sort of crazy sometimes, a girl of fifteen cavorting like a child. And now racing into the wind with her pale hair streaming, running like a wild thing. Away from books and stuffy old geometry, perhaps away from growing up. She could not have told anybody why she ran. She could not have put into words how life was pushing her on, pulling her back, sending her in a thousand confusing directions now here and now there.

These days it was really only when alone on the beach

that Minna felt sure of herself, here on her own ground among the eternities of sand and sea and sky. They always had a calming influence, even on days like this. They were here before there were any people, and would still be here after the last man. Only it would probably be a last woman, Minna thought. Women had so much more staying power than men. But it was awesome, really. For thousands of years, even millions, the tides had gone out and come back, bringing the waves to dash against the cliff and carve weird sculptures. The houses that now stood so proudly on the heights might one day fall into the sea as it steadily ate into the land; they might be swept away to other shores where other girls like Minna would wonder where the pieces had come from as they gathered the bits of flotsam for firewood.

Dragging behind her several timbers encrusted with the lavender patterns of what looked like miniature volcanoes and actually were barnacles, Minna trailed at last slowly up the steep steps that led away from the beach, conscious that it must be getting late. It was the end of her brief hour or so of freedom. Tomorrow, no, even tonight—she would be back in shoes again, confronted by all the problems and complications of having to grow up. They wanted you to grow up and act like a lady, and then they took it for granted that you'd happily accept the invitation to be a darn childish Grunion again in the Carnival! Her grievance came back to her, fresh as when new.

Yet, suppertime lights were glowing along the narrow

tree-shaded street that led home; she was good and late. With her load and her reluctance she was moving at the pace of a snail—naturally a sea snail, or limpet. On either side of her, flowers banked the lane, flowing down the banks in colors dimmed in the twilight but still in riotous pastel. It was a land that knew no real winter, a land aflame with bougainvillaea and geraniums, the air fragrant with year-round roses, and acacias.

Minna paused at her own gate to admire the outline of their house against the violet sky, the fading sunset streaks of scarlet and gold. Rambling and irregular, covered with weathered shingles, gray smoke rising from its chimney, the house tonight was the very picture of what ecstatic tourists were wont to call "real old Cliffside charm."

"And often accompanied by termites," her father said when he overheard them.

The timbers she was carrying dropped with a clatter on the woodpile, and Minna slipped through the side door that led directly to her bedroom. Mother might fuss because of her tardiness, but in this house there was one hard-and-fast rule that could not be defied. There could be no beachcombers at Mother's table. Minna hastily slipped into a corduroy jumper and slicked back her hair, wishing as always that it was one shade blonder. Then she descended upon the dining room.

"Minna, have you no idea of time?" Mother looked up impatiently at her entrance, but Father smiled approval. He liked to see her with her face flushed by sea and fresh air, he always said.

"Sorry, Mom, I'll try to do better. But the time goes so fast—"

"You ought to get a sundial and carry it with you at all times," said Father. "You did keep us waiting, chick."

"Truly, I'll try to remember next time." Minna was always sincere in her promises, but she was always finding out that no matter how good the intentions, promises were hard things to keep. She realized that her hands, even in the soft candlelight, were faintly grubby, and she was grateful when Mother turned her full attention upon the souffle. To Minna the dish tasted just like scrambled eggs with spinach, and what earthly difference did it make whether it was "fallen" or not when it was all the same anyway down in your stomach?

"It wouldn't have happened if it hadn't been for your tardiness, dear," said Mother, being the martyr. Minna couldn't help feeling that she was the squeak in the machinery of an otherwise well-run household.

"Okay, okay," said Father. "She's here now, isn't she?"

"So Father's home from the hardware emporium and Mother's home from the gift shop, and the sailor's home from the sea," Minna said with her best smile. "Only I didn't sail very far out today. Everything tastes awfully good, Mom."

"At your age you always have an appetite," said Mother. But she seemed somewhat pleased.

Which Minna wasn't, not at all. Suddenly it all came back to her. "I'm so mad I could spit!" she announced.

"Minna Vail!" said her mother.

"Well, I am! What do you think? Mrs. Latham called up this afternoon, just when I got home from school. And they want me to be a Grunion again. I'm sick and tired of being a Grunion! That's for *children!*"

"Well, for heaven's sweet sake, what are you?" That was Father.

"Why worry yourself about it now, dear?" Mother took a practical view, as usual. "The Carnival of the Sea is months away, and your dinner is getting stone-cold."

But by now Minna's face was clouded, and she was in no mood to eat any old dinner. Why did everyone always think of her as the Grunion type? "She knows her onions about the Grunions!" If her father made his favorite quip again about her usual role in Cliffside's annual summer carnival, she'd scream! Right out loud, and right this minute!

But instead he said gravely, "What's so wrong about being a Grunion, if I may ask? They're an interesting phenomenon of this southern California coast; they make their runs in few other places. People come for miles and miles—"

"Silly little fish, dancing on their tails!" Minna forestalled a possible dissertation by her father on the subject of icthyology. And all of this had nothing to do whatever with her again being the leader of the Grunion troupe. Dressing up in silvery tights, running around through the crowds of visitors and handing out souvenirs, turning handsprings, altogether making a fool of herself in public, was all so childish that she almost choked with righteous indignation. It wasn't—it wasn't ladylike.

How she behaved in private on a lonely beach was quite another affair. Besides, nobody saw her. But didn't anybody, even her own parents, stop to remember that she was fifteen years old, and more? A girl going on sixteen certainly was a different person from a mere child of fourteen; there was a world of difference. She had a new perspective about many, many things, not only just about this silly, perfectly absurd Grunion routine.

"It's time I was a Mermaid!" There now, she'd said it; she'd come out with the secret wish she hadn't intended to reveal, at least not yet. "I'm too grown-up to be a cute little kiddie any longer. I want—I want to be a little glamorous! Is that so funny?"

Mother was smiling into her napkin, but Father was less restrained. "My gracious! I suppose you want to wear a Bikini suit and appear on television, like your cousin Lucia! And as for a Mermaid, you haven't the figure for it. I tell you right now, young lady, I wouldn't trade you as you are for a dozen of those precious kittens up in Beverly Hills, playing rock'n roll records all night and sleeping till noon, with their eyebrows plucked and their mouths painted up like circus clowns—"

They were about to get into a real family argument, Minna could see that and Mother probably could, too. Father had been given an opening for one of his favorite lectures, the topic: Girls Should Act Their Age. They shouldn't try fancy rinses on their hair even if their hair happened to be naturally just an off-shade of blond; they shouldn't use any make-up except just a trace of lipstick maybe. He couldn't stand girls who looked as if they were made up for the musical comedy stage or the television camera. "All this eye shadow, so they look as if they'd run into two doorknobs!" He was warming up. "I'll not have a daughter of mine dripping with mascara and barn paint, looking cheap!"

Father was a double-duck, a dear, and Minna adored him fervently. But you had to admit he was dreadfully old-fashioned about a lot of things. He seemed to live in the remote past, and he had a list as long as your arm, or maybe both your arms, of Do's and Don't's for Growing Girls. And he never seemed to be aware that whether he liked it or not, his darling little girl was out of pinafores and middy blouses.

Minna had not, to tell the truth, even experimented with most of the cosmetics he kept mentioning. And if Father had his way she would go to her grave without knowing if a faint green or purple shadow would make her eyes mysterious. "A natural-looking girl is a pretty girl!" was his general idea. "Soap and water!" No nonsense about exotic perfumes either. Only toilet water was on his Christmas list, preferably something called *Sweet Lavender* or *Old Rose Garden* when what any girl actually yearned for was *My Sin* or *Indiscreet.*

Had Father ever really *lived?* Had Mother never tried mysterious lures and charms on him, not ever even in the beginning? Little did poor Father know what girls were in the habit of using, then as now. From his remembered version of their courtship, it had all been done with the ukulele and strains of the Charleston and the scent of good old Pear's Soap. Never in his life had he caught as much as a sultry whiff of *Black Narcissus* or its like, according to him. Mother smiled and said nothing.

Minna waited until Father paused for breath, and then seized the opportunity to cut him off the air by beginning to clear the table without being told. And she announced that she had loads of homework; perhaps dear Daddy would help her later with her Latin, which was all Greek to her. Somehow she had to switch his mind off modern youth and its failings.

"I do like to see a girl helping her mother without being told half a dozen times!" He beamed at her as she stacked up the dishes, carried them to the kitchen, and began to make suds in the sink. But her main idea at the moment was to get the chore done in the shortest possible time and then call up Laura. Best friends were often really the only ones you could talk to at times like this.

"Want to wipe, Dad?" she grinned invitingly at him. It was an old joke between them; Father hated dishes as much as cats hate water. Whenever she or Mother hinted about getting one of those automatic dishwashers he was always installing for his customers, though, he would only wince and then hastily suggest using paper plates. "I'm a man of simple tastes," he was fond of saying.

Simple or not, he had tonight messed up three china plates, a gold-threaded mat, and left cigar ashes in his coffee cup. Mother prided herself on setting an attractive table, trying out colors and combinations and ideas that she could use later in her gift shop displays. It was impossible to imagine Mother ever agreeing to use paper plates except for a picnic. Mother was conventional, and she was going to be no help at all about this Grunion problem. She would point out that the judges would never think of selecting Minna, a mere child of fifteen, for a Mermaid! Whatever in the world did she have to offer, in face or figure, in competition with the loveliest young ladies in all Cliffside and the surrounding country?

Minna dejectedly washed the same dish over and over, feeling very sorry for herself. It was awful to have to be just Minnow Vail, that flat-chested, skinny little runt whose father wouldn't let her wear any make-up except lipstick, and for even that she had had to fight a battle with Mother's help. Mother had been wonderful then. "I have noticed that all the girls use lipstick," she had pointed out at the time when Minna had entered high school. "You don't want our daughter to look different from the others, do you? It's not a sign of moral degradation, not in this century."

But the trouble was, Minna needed more than just lipstick. Looking at herself in the mirror over the sink, she almost cried in despair. So far as she could see at the moment, she had not so much as the beginning of one single beauty feature. Her eyes were too big and starey for her small face, her chin was too square, her ears stuck out too far. As for her fair complexion and her silky honey-color hair, anyone could achieve that with a foundation make-up and a rinse. Nor was there anything about her figure to beat the drums about, at least not yet. Though she had hopes in that direction; she was still growing.

But not fast enough! Why, oh why, did life have to be so complicated? Why did you always have to sigh for what was beyond your reach? Minna stood on tiptoe to hang up the copper frying pan in its place on the wall among the fish molds. Life wasn't anywhere near as easy as it had been. It couldn't be arranged and put in order in a few minutes, like this neat, cozy kitchen.

Am I doomed to be a wallflower? she asked herself. No boy had ever asked her for a date, and she wouldn't know what to do if one ever did. Staring at the pattern of the flowered curtains, Minna suddenly wanted to cry, though that was foolish and made your eyes all red. She was ashamed of these storms that came across her like squalls over the surface of the sea, but sometimes she felt as though she had lost her rudder and was drifting in the trough of the swells.

Minna wasn't a child any more, but she was not yet what anybody was ready to consider calling a woman. She could not sail her course by the old charts, and she had not found a new one.

The books and the magazine stories about such things couldn't help her. No one could help her—not even Mother and Dad, though heaven knows they tried. But they had forgotten how it was to be young, always too young for what you wanted to do. A girl had to figure it out somehow for herself. Right now she felt dreadfully alone. And wasn't she feeling sorry for herself, though! You'd think she had lost her last friend, and that she was an orphan standing out in the snow and trying to sell matches! I must look as melancholy as one of those basset hounds, Minna thought suddenly. And she had to smile at the thought. Thank goodness the muley-grubs moods passed almost as quickly as they came.

The dishes were done, too. She found herself whistling, a supposedly unladylike but very comforting ability she had acquired last year. "So here go all the boys I know, and the darn old Carnival committee, too!" she made pretend as she disposed of the garbage. "Who cares? They're not worth worrying about!" In a minute she would be talking to Laura on the phone, and her bosom friend would surely agree with her. On the other hand, Laura might be as hard to convince as Minna was herself, deep down inside.

2

New Boy!

As soon as Laura answered, Minna carried the instrument into the clothes closet, her private telephone booth. A girl needs privacy. Now Laura's parents took a sensible, progressive attitude about such matters; they let their daughter have her own phone in her own room. And—crowning touch—it was red! "Colored phones are just another of those phone company promotion gimmicks," Mr. Vail had scoffed when Minna told him about this exciting, wonderful Christmas present. "I suppose the next thing the Adamses will do is get a phone for their dog!"

So it was that now, while Minna crouched uncomfortably among coats and boots and old tennis rackets, her dearest friend could sprawl in ease across the bed, probably eating chocolates, too. There was a squish in her voice; it would be chocolates or caramels. Laura was supposed to be dieting again, but she had a secret hoard on hand.

"Don't talk to me about Grunions," Laura was saying. "The very thought of *anything* to eat makes me ravenous!"

But all the same she listened, not unsympathetically, to her friend's tale of woe—as if she had not heard it many times before in other variations. Laura was something of a philosopher. Yes, it wasn't easy to be fifteen, and maybe the best thing to do *was* to stop struggling. "You're always too fat or too thin or too noisy or you don't get outdoors enough or you don't read the right things," she admitted. "You always think the world is watching you, and maybe it is when you don't want anybody to, and you get so confused you can't even pull the right bar on the candy-bar machine. You get something with peanuts in it." Laura's thoughts ran strictly along the lines of something to eat. It was a real tragedy when you put in your dime and got a peanut bar instead of the almond-and-coconut marvel you had your heart set on.

The discussion rambled on, finally coming around to the possibility of embracing eternal spinsterhood as the easiest and simplest way out. They would join the sorority of old maids with which Cliffside, like most resort towns, abounded; they would have six or seven cats and collect antique glassware.

"And furniture," Minna said. "Highboys, very old and very rich."

"You take the highboys and I'll take the *low* boys!"

"And you come right out of that closet, Miss Minna Vail!" Mother suddenly flung open the door and extracted her with a firm hand. "Once you get started on that phone, you'll hang on until you die of old age—or downright suffocation!"

"May Day—gotta go now!" shouted Minna into the phone. After she had hung up she collected her mind, trying to think of some other valid excuse for not starting her homework. But, racking her brains, she could think of none that stood a chance. If she said it was too chilly to stay in her room, Mother would have her bring everything out and study on the dining-room table, practically under her eyes. That meant really sweating it out; there would be no dawdling and no daydreaming. Well, what had to be had to be.

She climbed into her old flannel bathrobe and the big furry slippers that resembled twin rabbits, thinking as she did so that one could practically freeze to death in California at night just as easily as back in Illinois. It seemed that way, anyhow. Her father was always reading the paper and quoting how it was below zero in Devil's Lake, North Dakota, or somewhere; you'd think he was on the Chamber of Commerce or something.

Having settled the weather problem for now, Minna turned cautiously toward her books. There was nothing for it now but to begin tomorrow's Latin assignment—another page of translation from *Caesar's Commentaries*. How could military campaigns be so dull? The Roman legions were always building walls or digging ditches or surrounding the enemy in a tiresome and repetitive fashion, but it was all ancient history. Didn't they ever take time out to storm walled cities and then just take them over for an evening's fun like the marines in training down at Camp Pendleton? Some weekends the marine recruits—"gyrenes" they liked to call themselves—would come roaring into Cliffside on a weekend and make the place jump with jive, to the open delight of the younger set and the disdain of the adults.

Now if Caesar ever told what his soldiers did in their spare hours besides polishing their shields, she hadn't come to that part yet. "If I could only wait and see the movie," Minna said to herself and giggled. But Caesar didn't have to worry about what Minna's composition teacher called "reader interest." He had a captive audience; he could bore you as much as he liked and you had to translate him or you flunked. It was as simple as that.

The Roman girls looking up at her from the illustration on the opposite page had never had this problem, Minna thought ruefully. Latin was their language, and they spoke it practically from the cradle. They could spend their evenings practicing on the lyre or taking graceful poses. To judge by the look of them, here in the pictured frieze, they had never been awkward, never had had what Mother called "growing pains." They could run around in lovely flowing draperies that probably never needed buttons sewed on them. And they could wear sandals instead of ugly sensible loafers—which reminded Minna that hers needed cleaning. No wonder the Roman girls looked so happy and carefree. How simple everything was back in those times! Minna caught herself. She had wasted so much time on idle speculation that she'd barely scratched the surface of her homework. Well, tomorrow in study hall she would have to make up for lost time.

Study hall was a place where, if you didn't have any boys to send notes to, you could really dig down and concentrate. Being a sophomore did have certain advantages, if you could call them that. Nobody noticed you much. Unlike the seniors, you had no long list of achievements that were supposed to make others stand in awe of you. And last year, as a bewildered freshman, you made so many mistakes you were always conspicuous. . . .

Like this boy sitting across the aisle. He looked old for a freshman, but the green cap thrust in his pocket was a dead giveaway. This close to the beginning of the semester, freshmen always had to have their green caps with them, the little red button on top being a further badge of their low degree. "Button, frosh!" How often Minna had heard this command from an upper classman when her arms were just overflowing with books. You had to drop everything and press the top of your head or pay a penalty!

This boy's legs were so long they reached to the next seat, and unless the light deceived her, he had the beginnings of a beard. You could tell by his scowl that nothing was pleasing him. "What's bugging you?" Minna risked a whisper and the possible rebuke from Mr. Abrams up front. "Old Ironsides," as he was called behind his back, was supposed to have radar ears that could hear a bobby pin drop a block away.

The boy shook his head and held up a card that read, "I am a Foreign Exchange Student. I do not speak your language well." Minna was suddenly intrigued. Now what country did he come from? He was so obviously ill at ease that she decided a little friendly ribbing might help. All right, so he was an exchange student. But where from? He looked—well, he looked *foreign* but nothing that she could immediately put her finger on. Choosing the least possible derivation that she could think of, she sketched a face with exaggerated slant eyes and a parasol with a big exaggerated question mark.

No, he wasn't a Japanese. As she held up the sketch, the boy even had the beginnings of a grin as he shook his head. She pondered over what to use to represent India? Of course—a snake charmer in a turban, sitting cross-legged. The snake wasn't very snaky, but her art had an appreciative audience. Africa, then. A palm tree and a giraffe. No dice. Was he from Scandinavia, maybe? She sketched a skier whizzing down a mountain. That could stand for Switzerland, too, but—

The strange boy had taken up a pencil and was drawing with furious speed. It was a windmill and a bed of tulips and his name was Hans Van Der Oster, as she could make out in a script so precise and so beautiful that it looked as though he had engraved it.

The next move was up to her, so she wrote "Greetings, Hans." The only way she could say it in the funereal silence of the study hall was to clasp one of her hands in the other and shake it, prize-fight style. "Greetings!"

She would certainly have a lot to tell Laura when she met her and the rest of the sophomore crowd at lunch time. They had all brought theirs in paper bags—the usual. Pickles, tuna fish sandwiches, peanut butter with jelly, potato chips, with milk on the side. You could buy the milk from the vending machine and then carry it out to the table underneath the eucalyptus trees. The noon sun warmed the leaves and filled the air with their spicy, medicinal aroma; as Betty Kent said, when you smelled the eucalyptus oil you almost felt you had a cold and somebody had put on the vaporizer.

"Not that anyone ever has a cold; not in California." Ciss Hunter sneezed into her cleansing tissue. "It's practically unpatriotic, my dad says so. So I guess that I just got me an allergy."

This particular table, located as it was a respectful distance from those now occupied by juniors and seniors, was almost always available. Here under the trees it often was decorated with droppings from the birds, and no one but sophomores could possibly want it. As for the freshmen, they had to eat on the steps that led to the dining terrace, a tradition long preserved and strictly enforced. Hans Van Der Oster probably didn't know about this, Minna thought. Somehow she hoped the foreign boy with the bony face and the reluctant smile wouldn't appear and park where he shouldn't, and then be hurt and embarrassed.

As usual, to hear them tell it, each of the girls had had a perfectly ghastly morning. No one ever admitted that it could have been otherwise. It wasn't the thing to do; you made the most of your difficulties, building them up for all they were worth. Your friends suffered for and with you. You had gotten up late, missed the school bus, and had to tramp all the way up the hill. Only some parent had taken pity on you and given you a ride and then the car had run out of gas or something. You had to make a run for it and reached your assembly room just as the last bell rang. How you ever managed it nobody would ever know, least of all Minna—who was the heroine of this particular tale of woe, and to top it all had broken a shoelace. "I was fit to be tied—only it wasn't!" she said, waiting for a laugh. Now that you were a sophomore you could laugh about anything, even the things that had seemed so tragic a year ago, especially if you made up a good story about them. It was good to be sitting among friends out under the eucalyptus trees.

Betsy was a clown, now re-enacting a gooey, passionate love scene she had seen last night on television. She was a born mimic but too shy to perform before any but her intimates. And Ciss was urging everyone to go with her to the movies tonight, which was a Friday. "They're drawing names for the jackpot, and one of us might win.

Somebody has to—I mean, somebody from Cliffside. They can't *always* be drawing the name of somebody who lives in another town and isn't in the theater. Gosh, just think of winning all that lovely money!" Her blue eyes sparkled as though she could already hear her own name being called.

The girls pondered the prospect, savoring its delicious possibilities, and then Betsy added fuel to the burning desire in each heart by saying that her mother knew a woman in Arizona who had won one hundred dollars the very first time she tried! Because of their small size, she and Minna could get in for half price as under twelve if they didn't wear lipstick.

"No," said Minna firmly.

"Oh, don't be stuffy. Everybody does it if they can."

"Well, I don't. Not any more. My father says—"

"Look, Minnow—you just don't want to pass for a kid, even to save twenty-five cents! Who's getting to be a young lady so sudden?"

Minna wondered if perhaps that was partly true. She found herself wondering about so many things these days. But anyway, she was not going to save a quarter, not that way.

"I get a dollar for every half pound I lose!" Laura's dark eyes were hopeful. "And if I weigh myself before dinner tonight I just possibly might make it." Betsy was baby-sitting tomorrow for the lady next door, and they might give her her pay in advance if she asked them. Minna herself had been collecting empty Coke bottles as an essential part of her beachcombing operations, and after school this afternoon she might be lucky enough to locate a few more half buried in the sand to lug back to the store for the legitimate deposit loot. Ciss was the only one who was sure of her funds; decisive and thrifty, she never overspent her allowance, never borrowed. But sometimes she would lend. Anyway, there would have to be a lot of phoning and checking and rechecking among the girls before the movie box office opened tonight. They almost always traveled, some of the mothers pointed out, like a flock of birds.

Minna had been holding back her own news until the last. Sooner or later the talk usually got around to the topic of boys, and she felt that at last she had something to say on the subject. "You couldn't exactly call him cute," she said, trying to describe Hans. "He's—well, there's too much of him for that. And he's *older*. Seems more of the strong, silent type. His hair is almost no color at all, and it hangs over his eyes. I bet he'd look better with a crew cut. But his face has lots of planes and lines and character, and he smiles unexpectedly."

There were the proper responses from Laura and others, but Betsy was unexpectedly full of pertinent information. "Why, he must be the boy who's staying with the Schmidts up on Loma Drive," she cried. "Mrs. Schmidt was telling my mother. They didn't exactly want him, either—they're too old to have young people around. But he's a cousin, or a cousin of a cousin, or something. They're doing it as an obligation or something."

"Can't be much fun for him," Minna said. "No wonder he looks so down-beat. I don't think he likes America one small bit. Or much of anything or anybody in it, either." It must really be awful to be far away from home, Minna thought, and in a strange school. And having to stay with an old couple like the Schmidts who went to bed every night at nine o'clock and who just couldn't *stand* noise.

"They're so old they're practically dinosaurs." Betsy was enlarging upon the topic of the moss-bound Schmidts. "You know, the kind that drive their old heap like the speed limit was ten miles an hour. What a taste of American family life that poor kid must be getting!"

When the bell suddenly rang for afternoon classes, Minna's thoughts were anywhere but on geometry. She couldn't help thinking about Hans and wondering whether in Holland—no, the Netherlands—boys and girls even went to the same schools. He had seemed so surprised, almost shocked, when she had whispered to him. Maybe back home girls didn't do such things without a formal introduction. *"Fräulein* Vail . . . *Herr* Van Der Oster, and how do you do . . . ?" all the while bowing from the waist and maybe even getting your hand kissed.

It might be hard for him to learn American ways, but at least he could start by dressing like the other boys in high school. The Schmidts should help him with that, but probably they were so out of date they didn't know that a boy looked odd in school wearing a suit and a white shirt and a necktie. You only did that when you were going to graduate or take a girl to a dance.

Looking around the classroom, she noted the baggy corduroys and faded blue-jeans, the grubby sweat shirts and the T-shirts and the loud plaids that made up the typical boy's uniform at Cliffside High. They were a sloppy-looking crowd, now that she tried to look at them through the eyes of a stranger. Most of them wore sneakers, and even the ones who wore loafers scorned ever to shine them. You could take any of them for young hoboes if you didn't know better; not one looked as if he had a thin dime.

The American high school had laws that were never to be found in Euclid, and Minna already knew that the very first one was "Don't dare to be different!" Hans would have to learn this for himself, and soon, if he wanted to be happy here.

"Minna! Are you still with us, Minna?" The teacher's voice cut into her reveries with a sharpness that made her realize she must have missed his question. What in the world had it been? What had he been asking her? She hated to be singled out, made to feel conspicuous—like a sort of oddball.

"What is the axiom that applies to problem three on page sixteen of your text—if you've bothered to open it?" Mr. Brown could be stingingly sarcastic when he wanted to be.

"Yes, it's—ugh—" She hadn't the slightest idea of the answer. Frantically she looked across several aisles in the direction of Bob Jones. He was a skin-diving pal of hers.

And, what was more important now, the smartest boy in the class. With a barely perceptible gesture, he slipped all but three fingers down from one of the hands that cupped his cheek while the other remained in position.

"Wh-why, the whole is equal to the sum of its parts. Axiom eight, of course."

"Very good. Minna, you surprise me. The problem was intended to mislead, but I'm glad to see that at last you're beginning to get a certain grasp. . . ."

Bob had saved her again, but as she hastened to thank him after class, he was surly about it. "Do your own studying, girl. You've got to develop your mind *some-time*."

"Which is tough for me, Bob. You know it is. I do try. But today I was thinking about something else."

"With what?" He could be obnoxious, more so than any other boy she knew. "With which of your two little pointy heads, huh?"

"I was going to ask you another kind of favor, but I guess that's all for today"—she had her pride—"if that's the way you're going to act." It wasn't for herself. It had been for Hans. She wanted Bob to invite the Dutch boy to come down to the shore tomorrow, to the beach where everyone went to watch the surfers riding on their boards, or more likely falling off them. Hans might enjoy that, and it might give him a chance to get better acquainted with the crowd.

Not that Minna was interested in him as a boy, she told herself firmly. Only as a person who very likely was sick—

homesick. She had been away at summer camp one year, and she knew what that was—an ache that went all over you. "Oh, Bob!" she cried, suddenly changing her mind and running after him down the crowded hall. "Bob!"

3

Friday Night

"Doing anything special tonight, Dad dear?" Minna sauntered into the living room, her movie money at last in her pocket. As always, it had come hard. Besides her hoard of soft drink bottles retrieved from the beach and from the picnic grounds near it, she had sold several dozen of the starfish she had pried from the rocks at low tide and sun-dried in the special area in the yard reserved for her varied marine collections. Well, it wasn't exactly *reserved;* Mother used the same spot for hanging out the laundry when she could work her way in around the driftwood.

Mother had small appreciation for the grotesque shapes of twisted, water-worn shapes that were among her daughter's treasures. She did not seem able to see in them the forms of dragons, horses, monsters—nor did she appreciate the others grayed by the eternal sea and patterned with tiny white shells. These could, in financial extremity, be sold to one of the local florists as the base for floral arrangements. This was wood definitely not *ever* to be burned.

Father put aside the local paper, which came out just once a week, to make a place for her on his lap. "Are you asking the old man for a date?"

"I'm glad I'm not too big to be held," she said as she snuggled down. It was pleasant here by the stone fireplace, with the warm glow of the flames beating upon her face, with Father's arms about her and delicious smells eddying from the kitchen. A picture, she thought tenderly—even with that dear old reprobate of a tomcat dozing before the hearth. Minna found herself swept with a deep feeling of contentment. She loved her home, and she loved Mom and Dad. She would never, never leave it and them; she never wanted to grow up and go away. . . .

Except tonight, and just to the local movies. "You will drive us all, won't you Dad?" she implored him later, across the dinner table. He was always most amenable when fed. "The Kents will pick us all up afterwards."

"When did I ever do anything else on a Friday night but take you somewhere, young lady?" He put on his patient, long-suffering parent look.

"There *was* a time. . . ." Mother dimpled prettily at him across the table. They were *people!* Minna realized suddenly. Parents were actually people, sweethearts, lovers. Even at their age! Absorbed in one's own affairs, you were apt to forget that fact. Their personal, private lives weren't really over at all. Sometimes you caught glimpses, and then drew back a little bit embarrassed, as though you had looked into somebody else's diary or peeked into a window. "The dears," she thought. "I bet they're still even a little bit in love."

Being Minna, her thoughts jumped elsewhere. She was popping the corn tonight to take with them to the show. And Laura was making fudge. The girls' finances would stretch only to cover the price of admission, and did not include store-bought refreshments. If you got thirsty, you went and got a drink of water out of the fountain in the foyer; you didn't go for that orange-drink stuff that tasted like acid water with stale ice in it. Of course if you were out with a boy and he showed off and bought it for you, you would pretend that you enjoyed it. You had to, when it cost fifteen cents for a small glass and a whole quarter for a large one.

Out with a boy! Lots of girls no older than Minna were standing in line before the box office right now tonight, arms linked with a real live boy, a temporary but much-prized possession. It went on all the time. If you didn't go to the movies, especially on Friday evenings, you didn't know who was dating whom. It was far more accurate than the gossip column in the high school paper. Why, you even saw some of the little kids from junior high coming to the movies in couples. "And I'm sure I don't know what their parents are thinking of!" Mrs. Vail would say, as she and Dad drove up to let off Minna and her crowd.

News of the jackpot giveaway had brought a varied turnout, young and old; even senior citizens were here to try their luck, in spite of the main feature which was something called *Nights on the Nile* and not their cup of tea at all, judging by the ads. Minna, glancing curiously at the queue in front of the ticket window, spotted Hans Van Der Oster escorting old Mrs. Schmidt, looking, as usual, neat and stiff and a little bewildered. It couldn't be such a lot of fun for him, Minna thought sympathetically, pointing him out to her friends.

"You can have him, you saw him first," Laura said airily. "He looks squarer than square." Then she gasped, looking up into the face of one of last season's football heroes, who had just trodden heavily on her foot. "It's nothing, nothing at all!" she cried with enthusiasm. "I really don't mind a bit!"

"Uh-huh!" thought Minna. Probably dear Laura would wear a bandage at school Monday, hoping the big man on campus would remember and notice her. Anything for an excuse for further conversation if they just accidentally on purpose happened to meet in the hall.

Now at last they were inside. Laura always wanted to sit in the back where they could watch the couples come in, but Betsy was nearsighted. So, as usual, they compromised by settling down somewhere toward the middle of the house, keeping as far away as possible from a noisy raft of grammar school boys who were already catcalling and stamping their feet, impatient for the picture to begin. "Who let them out of the zoo?" Ciss said in a loud stage whisper. All the girls were conscious of their sophomore dignity and superiority.

"What if one of *them* wins the jackpot?" Betsy giggled.

"He'd probably spend it all on bubble gum." This was from Laura, who had a younger brother and *knew*.

As the house lights finally dimmed for the picture, Minna thought that she caught a glimpse of no less than George Hartford, who'd lived across the street from her as long as she could remember. He was supposed to be away at UCLA now, but he could have come home for the weekend. Anyway, if it was George he had brought a girl with him, a girl with fluffy pale hair and one of those new bulky coats Minna had seen featured in the fashion pages in her mother's magazines. George was always falling in love with girls who seemed to come from another world, a world of soft, flattering lights and dancing and—well, a world beyond imagining. She tried and tried to recall a phrase from a fashion ad that had caught her fancy. "Airy sophistication," that was it. Minna sighed. How very wonderful to be such a fashion-ad girl, in a coat like that, and to have George Hartford in love with you!

Last year, as a high school senior, he had seemed unattainable, remote, but ever desirable. He moved in that special aura of glory which, in a humble freshman's eyes, touched this exalted class. Now that he had actually gone away to college, he was even farther out of her reach, out of her sphere. It didn't matter that Minna's brother, now a junior at the same university, should write him off as "that Hartford punk." Or that George himself should refer to her—and she had heard him—as "that little twerp across the street." Someday, she thought—someday he would think otherwise about her—so her secret dreams went. And she was more than willing to worship him from a distance.

The extravaganza they were watching on the screen was laid in ancient Egypt and had been shot on location there according to the movie magazines. There was a slave girl, who happened to be more beautiful than the queen even in her simple garments of unbleached cotton. All the ladies of the court were jealous of her, and they plotted to ship her off up the Nile to Nubia or Ethiopia or somewhere into desert wastes where there was nothing but sand and hyenas, whose howls sent chills up the spine.

The prince was furious when he returned home victorious over the Hittites or somebody, and he wormed the secret of the girl's disappearance out of the vizier and then hastened up the river in his barge hoping to be in time to save his beloved—for such he knew her now to be. And he really did pour it on the galley slaves.

"Get an outboard!" shouted one of the nasty little boys down in front.

"They did have sails in those days, didn't they?" Laura whispered to Minna, watching the poor men straining at the oars and making perhaps four knots an hour. The prince could have gone faster on foot, Minna thought. One of the galley slaves fell overboard and was immediately eaten by a crocodile, who didn't even shed any crocodile tears. Meanwhile, all sorts of things were happening or about to happen to the poor beautiful slave girl, who, if she escaped the fangs of the hyenas, seemed sure to perish of hunger and thirst.

The rich glittering jewels the prince was carrying to adorn her with wouldn't do her much good if he didn't hurry, and one thing after another got in the way to delay him. Besides, he didn't know that one of the jewel chests didn't contain precious stones at all, but had been filled with poisonous snakes! Asps, even!

Minna, who knew something of practical zoology, thought to herself that in actuality the big snakes would have eaten the smaller snakes and that besides they would all have smothered in the jewel chest for lack of air, but movies were movies. The wicked queen's henchmen were everywhere aboard, and it was really beginning to look bad for the slave girl even if she was still alive when they found her.

And then one night, when the prince was standing on the deck and watching the moon on the Nile, one of the evil henchmen loosed the top of the box—and suddenly a snake was out and slithering horribly across the deck, just as he cast himself despondently down on the royal cushions.

"Watch out!" Minna cried, in a voice so loud that it could be heard by everyone for rows around. Then she bit her lip. Everyone turned to stare at her and some tittered. Why, oh, why, had she had to go and act like a little kid? Her imagination was too vivid, and now she was perspiring with acute embarrassment as well as suspense. The drama had become so very real to her that she had identified herself with the beautiful slave girl. And the prince, of course, was George Hartford.

When at long long last the lights came on again, she was still lost in the ancient land of Egypt, caught in that last embrace, that last ardent kiss. "Must take a lot of practice," Ciss said irreverently. "I should think they'd run out of breath, those actors."

All eyes were fixed now on the stage, for what was to many of the audience the main attraction of the evening. The manager, who always wore a somewhat shabby tuxedo, was out on stage and after a few jokes and a little patter had called a youngster up from the front row to have the honor of drawing the first name slip from the whirling cylinder cage. Ciss said that the management kept the slips around for months; that was why there were so many of them. But Minna was paying little or no attention to the whirling of the so-called Barrel of Fortune, just at this moment.

Was it George Hartford down there toward the front, or wasn't it? Whoever it was had unobligingly turned his back to the aisle and was concentrating his entire attention on that girl with the platinum hair. She was wearing so much make-up you couldn't really tell what she looked like—eye-shadow, even!—but George, if it was George, seemed entranced.

"Will you stop leaning over me? I can't see what's

going on!" Ciss was impatient. "What in the world has gotten into you, Minnow?"

Minna subsided in her seat. She had had a good look, finally. And it hadn't been George, just somebody with a haircut like his. She was always making such mistakes, and it was foolish of her. Somebody walked like George, or swung his arms in the same way, or laughed the way he did . . . and her heart fluttered like a bird made captive. Only Laura was in on this thing about George—it was too precious a secret for Minna to share with anyone else but her one closest confidante. The other girls were always mooning over movie stars or television heroes, but Minna had a picture of George tucked away in her bureau drawer underneath all her sweaters. It wasn't really a picture that did him justice—just a newspaper clipping of a photo of George as newly-elected president of the senior class, somewhat fuzzy and blurred—but she would die if anyone but Laura ever saw it.

Now a name had been drawn for the first of the four twenty-five-dollar prizes, and everyone in the packed theater was tense and still. Even Laura had stopped munching popcorn. The girls were thinking in unison: what would it be like to win twenty-five dollars, the equal of six months' allowance? Think of the high heel shoes, the permanent waves, the manicures, the nylons, and the frilly lingerie that could be showered down by the hand of fate.

"Mr. John Holt!" boomed the manager's voice. "Is John Holt in the house?"

There was silence. "Will somebody repeat the name at the door in case he is outside?"

It was done, to no avail. And then suddenly the group of grammar school kids came alive with boiling commotion. Mr. John Holt turned out to be none other than Jackie Holt, aged nine, who had obviously never thought of himself as "mister" anything. Red as a beet with embarrassment, the small boy went bashfully up to claim his reward.

"What a waste, on a kid like that!" Ciss was indignant. "He'll just blow it all on ice cream and stuff. I hope he gets sick!"

There was no response whatever to the next two names drawn; they were absentees, probably from one of the neighboring beach towns, who would probably hear about it later and groan in misery. Or maybe they were people who didn't bother to come because they already had everything they wanted.

And then the last name to be drawn was a real disappointment. It was a well-dressed man, his dark suit and necktie proclaiming him a visitor. When he said his thanks he spoke in some sort of accent; maybe he was one of the winter tourists who came down from Canada. Obviously nobody who needed the money. Wouldn't you know? It was always like that. The girls looked at each other and sighed as one.

"We going to stay for the other feature?" Minna was getting restless, wriggling in her seat. It was hard for her to sit anywhere for four hours straight. But the others were adamant about staying, as they always were. Leaving a show before it was over—not getting one's full money's worth—was unthinkable. It would be a horrible extravagance.

And of course it gave them a legitimate excuse to stay out after twelve without being scolded. By that time the other movie had wound its way to a finish—it was a drama about a prize fighter who made a deal to throw a big fight and then changed his mind for love. When the girls came out, the little town would be different, and at its most glamorous. They would have to wait till Mr. Kent showed up, standing on the sidewalk outside the theater. Cliffside looked so intriguing at this time of night, with all the regular stores dark and deserted, and the neon lights at the hotel and the night spots flashing promises of forbidden gaiety and all the things that the town lacked by day. One felt somehow daring to be out after twelve, even standing safely under the marquee and then enclosed in the proper security of a parent's car. You were for that little while definitely "out on the town."

It was something Minna could look forward to, all through the prize-fight movie. On the whole it had been a pretty good evening, even if she hadn't actually seen George after all. And then something else happened. As she strolled out into the lobby to stretch her legs, she found Bob Jones standing treat at the water cooler with a crowd of other boys. "Hi, Minnow," he said, and offered her a paper cup full. "Dive in, it's about your size."

"Do you think you can spare it?" Minna said, she

was afraid not very brilliantly. She didn't think it was fair to tease a girl when she was outnumbered by so many members of the opposite sex.

"The Minnow's cute stuff when she gets mad, isn't she?" Bob was showing off, and she hated him cordially for it. She didn't relish being the main object of attention of half a dozen pairs of eyes, nor having Bob throw his arm about her shoulders as though she were—as though she were a hitching post! Didn't he know that a girl could have feelings, or didn't he care?

"I'll thank you to put your arm somewhere else, Mr.—Mr. Isosceles!" Her cheeks were suddenly aflame. "I don't like your angles."

The boys were still laughing as she hurried away inside to find her seat and watch the inevitable clinch of the prize fighter and his girl. Anyway, she had put Bob in his place. But he had called her "cute." She was nothing more than a swimming pal to him, that was the way he had always acted, but it hadn't done any harm to have the other boys hear him use that word.

4

A Real Surprise

You might call Bob "the typical American boy," Minna decided. She had paused to ponder while engaged in cleaning up her room—always a hated Saturday chore—to look through a pile of old magazines. Mother had put her foot down and said that she absolutely must throw some of them away; they were getting to be a disgraceful mess in that stack in the corner. But how on earth could a girl tell which ones she could consent to dump out unless she checked through them, every one?

You always found something interesting that you'd missed the first time around—like this survey, and the statistics on boys, illustrated with photographs for which Bob could have posed. Here was a short, stocky youth doing a handstand, his face peppered with "the cruel pimples of adolescence," as the article dramatically described them.

"At what age does the typical American boy begin to date?" Answer: "Fifteen or sixteen." "How does he show his first interest in girls?" Answer: "By teasing them, preferably before his peer group." Minna would have to look that one up in the dictionary, and she took the big volume from her desk. Mother would be impressed if she happened to look in, would think darling daughter was studying. And in a way she was; what more important subject could there be right now than boys?

> *Peer, n.* 1. A person of the same civil rank or standing; an equal before the law. 2. One who ranks with another in respect to endowments or other qualifications. 3. A nobleman.

This was certainly a way-out method of describing a gang of boys in a theater lobby, Minna thought. She went on to find out that the word "gang" was important, too, according to the magazine article. "The gang is an outgrowth of the boy's desire to identify himself with the group. It gives him a sense of social security."

Minna was absorbed. She supposed the same thing could be said for her own crowd of girls, and she couldn't wait to tell them. "I'm only identifying myself with you—" It sounded like the lyrics of a popular song.

"A girl of this age is more mature than a boy by several years, and while he confines himself to sports, she tries to lead him on into a more emotional response and a greater awareness of sex." Sex! For heaven's sake, they didn't have to get so serious about it, did they? Besides it didn't help to learn that boys were even more uncertain about this whole business of dating than she was. The way the magazine writer talked she should be practically ready to go out with George Hartford—and lead him astray!

Still, the magazine had given her a few clues, and she would not discard it. And from now on she might try to remember that when boys like Bob teased her or made her cross the poor immature creatures were only acting their age.

She realized that she hadn't half finished doing her own room, and she had also the kitchen floor to wash and half a dozen windows, too. Why, Saturday would be half over before she had completed the list of tasks Mother had made up for her to do before she had taken off for the gift shop. But still Minna dawdled. It was pleasant to have the big house all to herself—except for Peter, who had been rubbing against her legs a moment ago but now had disappeared. Probably into one of the bureau drawers, which she had been opening and closing in an effort to locate her bathing cap. He was always slipping into such cozy corners and going to sleep. When he woke up he would start yowling and protesting. She would have to locate him. With the weight of his years, which almost equaled her own, Peter needed to be pampered. If he were a man, he'd be senile and decrepit and close to a hundred! She found him in the linen closet, cradled him tenderly in her arms, and looked into the wise old eyes, the luminous amber depths. She wondered what secrets he could tell her if God had only granted him the gift of speech. Of course, he did have several different ways of saying "Mowrrr"—one for "out" and one for "hungry" and one for "I want to sit in your lap."

It was a shame to stay inside on a lovely day like this, she thought, going out into the yard to shake the dust mop and looking wistfully and tenderly across the street at the Hartford house. There was a chance that George might have come home for the weekend after all, but the windows of the room she knew to be his were closed.

"Any news, Mrs. Hartford?" she called to his mother, who had put on gardening clothes and was out clipping the hedge with the quick, impatient movements that were so like her son's.

"I guess not. Trust George not to be here when there's any work to be done," she said, but with a warm, indulgent note in her voice. "Do come over, Minnow—I want your mother to have some of my camellias." Mrs. Hartford made a hobby of raising these exquisite blooms. Now, as she filled a small basket with the perfection of flowers in shell pink and deep red and snowy white, Minna had to exclaim over them.

"Wow!" she said.

"You ought to be going to a party tonight, Minnow, so you could wear one in your hair." She chose one of the Lady Barbaras and tried the effect of the delicate pink against Minna's cheek. "A perfect match! You're getting to be a very pretty girl, my dear. Did you know that?"

"N-No," said Minna bluntly. "But it's awfully nice

of you to say so." This from George's mother! She might even mention it to him sometime. "Most of the time I just don't feel pretty at all, not a bit."

"What girls your age lack mostly is just self-confidence!" She cupped Minna's chin in her hand and made her look straight up at her. "I know I did, myself. And you only get it little by little." Mrs. Hartford had no daughters of her own, and now she put her arms around Minna. "Don't ever get discouraged, dear. We all went through it at one time or another. Personally, I don't see how we stood it. Now then," she gave Minna the basket and a friendly spank, "be off with you!"

Crossing the street and going down the flagstone steps, which were now warmed by the sun and pleasant to her bare feet, Minna went into the kitchen and took down one of her mother's large bowls. She arranged the camellias carefully, floating them on the water with a protection of waxed paper as Mrs. Hartford had once taught her to do, and hoped that Mother would be pleased. Darling daughter did not often take such an interest in table centerpieces, and search out candles in colors to match. But after what Mrs. Hartford had said, there was something different about these camellias, especially about the Lady Barbara. Clasping it in her hair with a bobby pin, she danced dreamily about the living room.

If someone let her use his surfboard this afternoon, which was possible but not likely, she would need one of her old sweaters. The water was cold in February; sitting out there among the breakers in a stiff wind, she did not especially care to freeze to death. No matter if she looked like an orphan ragamuffin in that torn sweater. When you fell off the board, you had to swim for it, and with the chance of its bouncing high and whacking you on the head, you had to be prepared to dive deep below the surface where the currents felt as though they had come straight down from the Arctic, special delivery.

What with one thing and another, Minna was late joining the throng from various high schools along the nearby Pacific coast, who were already gathered and waiting the turn of the tide. The beach at the foot of Bartholomew Street was practically covered with boys in swim trunks and girls in beach robes and all types of funny hats, so that at first she was at a loss to locate any of her own personal friends. They must be somewhere sprawled among all these blankets and mats and towels, somewhere amidst this cacophony of portable radios all tuned to different stations. Among them here and there lay the surfboards looking rather like great white fish left stranded on the sand. Some were being used as card tables and some for picnic lunches, but most owners frowned upon such desecration. Boys who were really serious about surfing spent hours putting various waxes and resins upon them, rubbing them down as tenderly as if they had been thoroughbred horses; a surfboard was a highly personal possession to be stood carefully against some rock until the right time came to launch it.

Even good friends seldom traded boards or loaned

them; and now, as Minna finally caught sight of Bob, she wished she had not come. He was standing in the surf holding his precious board for that girl from Latin class—what was her name?—who couldn't even swim worth a darn. "And so what do I do now?" Minna overheard her saying. It was hard to believe, but Bob was actually jumping on behind her and pushing her carefully out to sea! The two of them were acting as if they were on a joy ride or something.

"Showing off his big muscles, I suppose!" Minna said, half to herself, indignant at the times Bob had refused to let her take his board, saying that she might wreck it.

"Pretty silly, hey, Minnow?" That was Betsy's voice. Minna turned to find her crowd, hidden until now in a sheltered corner between the rocks and having a girl-party. Betsy was doing up her hair, Ciss was rubbing herself with tanning lotion, and Laura was engrossed in a magazine and a candy bar. It was a way of pretending that you didn't care a hoot about boys, and similar groups were scattered all about them. Like she-seals in a rookery, Minna thought.

Most of the young people who had assembled this Saturday afternoon had come to watch and be watched. They formed a gallery for the real surfers, who were beginning now to assemble where the waves formed for the long roll in to shore. Among her own group, Minna was the only one daring enough to try surfing when she had the chance, which was seldom. It was a difficult sport that took a great deal out of you; a girl was likely to be exhausted by the time she had paddled out far enough to catch the crest just before it broke and, standing up on the board, try to keep her balance for the long ride in to shore.

Mostly it was only the boys who surfed. And now, as Minna watched them starting to come in, she had to admit that they were far better at it than she was or probably ever would be. Probably because they all had their own boards and had nothing to do, it seemed, but to practice. They didn't have to spend the best part of Saturday cleaning up the house and scrubbing floors and windows. They had a head start. But adept as she was at most water sports, she hated to be outdistanced by boys, in any of them. It was a point of pride.

Also, it was a point of pride with her almost never to go to the beach dressed for swimming and then not go in the water, but today she hesitated. The sun had gone behind a cloud, the sea had lost its blue sparkle, and the wind was beginning to whip the sand with stinging force. Why get herself all wet and cold when other people were beginning to gather up their belongings and think about going home?

Yet Bob and his gang of boys had other ideas. Swooping down on her now, they seized her by the arms and legs and carried her kicking and screaming to the water's edge. She would not, she *positively* would not, be a good sport about it. They could have their childish fun with somebody else. As she struggled unsuccessfully to free herself, a boy's voice rang out, harsh with command. "Stop! Do not do that to a girl!"

Lo and behold, Hans Van Der Oster had appeared from somewhere to come militantly to her rescue! Bob must have invited him down, and now he was single-handedly defying the whole troop of them. But they took it easily. "Okay, Dutchie, if you say so! So it just isn't done that way in your country, huh?"

They dropped Minna unceremoniously on the sand, and immediately made Hans the victim of their horseplay. Swinging him back and forth, they sent him caroming out to sea in a mighty arc so that he landed flat on his back on the water. That could even stun a person, Minna knew; but Hans rolled swiftly and his arms were swinging in the powerful crawl of an experienced swimmer. Throwing himself forward on a wave then, he scudded onto the beach. Again his tormentors were upon him, but Hans was too quick for them. He dodged between a pair of legs, came up with a wrestling hold on their owner, and pinned him to the mat—or rather, to the ground. There was power in that thin gangling body of his, and he must have had some gymnastic training, too. Now that Hans, the stranger, had shown he was no coward and could not be pushed around or bullied, it all turned into good-natured fun, a tangle of arms and legs, as the lot of them tussled like a basket of puppies.

Minna wanted to stay and watch now, but her friends were shivering. "Did anybody say anything about a good hot drink?" Laura wanted to know.

Minna's house was closest to the beach, and they almost always stopped off there—for lemonade in summer, cocoa in winter. Cocoa! The woman in the picture on the cocoa can was Dutch, and that gave Minna an inspiration. Would it be all right to ask Hans to join them, or would he be embarrassed to be with so many girls at once? Suppose they couldn't talk to him, nor he to them? She voiced her doubts to her friends in a hasty, whispered consultation.

"Why, he's just a kid, like anybody else. I don't see why you have to make such a fuss about it." Ciss was getting impatient. "Ask him, or don't ask him. It's all the same to me."

Minna had wanted to make a friendly gesture, but she hadn't intended to overdo the "hands across the sea" bit. She had invited Hans, and he had somewhat stiffly and formally accepted. But the cocoa party wasn't too successful; Minna had had little experience at being hostess. Luckily Mother had come home before the group broke up and had invited Hans to stay for dinner.

"How is he going to get to know about a typical American home if he's never to spend any time in one?" Mother, cornered in the kitchen, thus countered Minna's protests. The Vails were hardly *adopting* Hans by just being hospitable, nor was there the slightest indication involved that Minna was trying to lure him into being her boy friend. Even if she wanted to practice, nobody would ever accuse her of starting out with a mere freshman. "He just seems like a very nice boy, that's all," said Mother.

So, this is why Minna was stuck with Hans Van Der Oster, playing a wild game of Chinese Checkers on a Saturday night, and trying to be gracious about it. Mother and Dad had gone out for the evening, Mother pointedly ignoring Minna's hint that they take Hans along in the car and drop him off at the Schmidts'. "She wants me to get used to seeing boys somewhere besides the beach," Minna said to herself, desperately wondering how you entertained a boy in the family living room.

It was medium ghastly. Without parental chit-chat to ease the tension, the two young people were stiff with one another. Minna had politely produced her high school annual, *The Cliffhanger,* from last year to show him, and he had politely thumbed through the pages. Then there was nothing but Chinese Checkers, though the game had always bored Minna to tears. She could not even be positive that the Hollander youth understood what she was trying to tell him about the rules of the game. He was so polite, so ready to nod and say Yes that she was sure he would have agreed with her if she had said that lemons with mustard sauce were delicious.

What to do? Perhaps he could dance—that would at any rate give them something to do besides just sit and talk. She hadn't danced, not with a *boy* as her partner, since her dancing school days years and years ago, but she and her girl friends were always practicing, taking turns leading each other. The steps would of course be strange to Hans, but that would be all to the good because then he would not notice how terribly awkward and uncertain she was.

Since the record player usually was loaded with her own collection of popular tunes, she did not bother to check the stack, and she was surprised when the first number turned out to be a tango, a haunting old number that begins *"Adios muchachos, companeros de ma vida. . . ."* She had seen the tango performed only in movies and on television, but to her it was a dream of beauty and romance and Latin rhythm; it was scarcely the type of dance anybody would attempt to do here in Cliffside. She was about to shut it off and try something else when Hans jumped excitedly to his feet.

"You know the tango, *ja?*" He was clicking his fingers enthusiastically, as though they were castanets.

"Me? Gosh, no!"

"I will show you, then." He held her lightly but firmly about the waist and moved slowly into the alluring South American rhythm, trying gently to force her into the difficult, formal steps. You bent backward at an impossible angle, you swayed your hips. . . . As Hans let her go for a moment and stood back to demonstrate, it all looked so easy and so wonderfully graceful! It might be far beyond her at the moment, but she could at least add one exotic touch that was in harmony with the romantic spirit of the moment.

Remembering the camellia, Minna stuck it behind one ear, with an exciting feeling that anything could happen next. The Saturday night had turned out wonderfully after all. Minna found out that the boy from the Netherlands, whom she hardly knew, danced like a professional, and now he had taught her the most glamorous of all ballroom dances!

5

Magic Morning

It had been one of those boring weeks at school when Minna felt she was on a treadmill that would last the rest of her life. No one had said or done anything amusing that she could recall; there had been several unexpected quizzes in which she had not distinguished herself; she was tired of all her clothes. . . . Altogether she was in the early-spring dumps. Most of her friends had guests coming down for the weekend from Los Angeles, or were going away with their families for a holiday in the desert. On Friday night Minna was indeed Miss All-Alone—and feeling very sorry for herself. The Vails scarcely ever went *anywhere*. With both Mother and Father in their separate businesses six days a week, they liked to stay close to home on their one day off. When their son Hugh finished college and had his teacher's certificate, it might permit them to take life a little easier.

Only when she was looking around the house for a newspaper in which to wrap the garbage did Minna begin to brighten. Articles about the ocean always attracted her attention, and now she was reminded by a one-column story that one of the lowest tides of the year was at hand. Saturday morning at six the sea would roll back and for a few all too brief hours reveal a wonderland. How very lucky that this was to happen on a weekend!

She would go to bed early and slip out the back door while everyone else in the house was still asleep. Mother wouldn't have a chance to warn her not to be too adventurous going far out on the slippery rocks, wouldn't worry about her dropping into chasms, being stung by a giant ray, or trapped by the sudden turn of the tide. To Mother's mind, the perils of the sea were a marine version of *The Perils of Pauline* as in the ancient movie serials.

The boy delivering papers along his route was the only person to see her emerge from the house early on that special morning. Wearing a heavy plaid shirt against the early chill, she ran on down past parked cars and fences dripping with sea mist. To the east, the low range of mountains beyond the town was in sharp silhouette against the brightening sky. As Minna turned a corner, she caught the first glitter of the sun. She was heading for a stretch of rocks that was never accessible except at these very low, neap tides; as she struck the clean-swept beach it was as though the whole world had just been created for her sole benefit. Everything was so fresh and new at this beginning of the day; no footprints showed upon the sand. She might have been the only human being alive here beside the pastel colors of the gentle sea.

Millions upon millions of years ago, creatures had first ventured from the mother sea to live on land; but Minna, trotting down the beach, was giving little thought to the concept of evolution as explained by her father. She only knew that she loved the sea, and the edge of the sea. She felt at home there. Whether it was due to a distant, atavistic memory or not mattered little on a morning like this.

Given her own free choice, perhaps she would have elected to stay in the ocean; she would like to be a dolphin or a porpoise. Three of these gay and friendly creatures were rollicking now not far from shore, leaping in a hop-skip-and-jump across the water and disappearing under the surface again with an effortless ease that left hardly a ripple.

There was no telling what one might see along the beach so early in the day, before humans had disturbed it. Perhaps, if she hurried, she might find a baby seal, as she had once done, cradled within a nest of sea weed and fast asleep. What a darling pet it would make, with its funny little head like a Teddy bear's, and its puppy bark. If she could capture it, not let it slither out of her arms. . . .

Now she was clambering over rocks slippery with sea-weed, the long graceful strands of what was so beautifully called "mermaid's hair," and over the luxuriant waste of kelp in whose forests of rubbery stems and leaves there was a veritable jungle in which the smaller creatures of the sea could hide from their myriad enemies. Here and there she skidded over bright green patches of moss, treacherous as soap, and then she was forced to balance herself against the living barnacles. Encrusting the rocks, they were as sharp as knives, and she was glad that she had worn her old tennis shoes instead of going barefoot as usual.

She went farther and farther out along the reef, leaping over the narrow channels that churned and foamed with the ceaseless and relentless surge of the sea. It would be unfortunate if she were to fall, all alone out here as she was, but she did not pause to think of that. Minna was drawn by the fascination of crystal depths that turned to indigo, by the darker passing shadows of what could be giant fish or marine monsters, by the entire compelling mystery of the sea.

As she ventured farther and farther out, the tide pools grew ever more fascinating. These cavities, revealed for only a few enchanting hours each spring and fall (at the season of the vernal and autumnal equinoxes) were the ocean's gardens, never stripped of their blossoms by casual beachcombers. Each was a little world in itself, and crouching low to look at them closely one could feel like some ancient pagan deity. If she sat quietly and did not stir even so much as a finger, all the creatures disturbed by her approach would gain courage and begin to scuttle or swim again about their business.

Tiny hermit crabs ran about with their houses on their backs; these were oddments of abandoned shells picked up here and there, and they looked like funny little hats. Rocks that had seemed bare suddenly were populated by larger crabs; in the crevices others lurked like bandits ready to pounce upon the unwary traveler of whatever sort of species—and eat him!

These were hungry worlds that Minna was studying; wary, cannibalistic worlds. The brownish blob remained a blob until it was sure the danger had passed. Then and only then would it thrust out the ears that gave it the name of sea hare and cruise sluggishly across the bottom of the pool. What had seemed to be merely a bump in the sandy bottom took form as a squid and jetted from one shadowy corner to another; it had a marvelous camouflage from its enemies. There could be real octopuses here as well, the tiny babies with tentacles only eight or ten inches long, who made the crevices under the rocks their nursery and playpen.

As always the turban shells and the limpets crawled slowly and steadily on their mysterious errands, entirely preoccupied with their own affairs, and probably unaware of the geometric perfection of their various forms. How intricately they were marked, how beautifully, too—and how frail they all seemed when one thought of them having to stand against the terrible force of the waves and currents when the sea came back!

As for the chitons, Minna had never seen one of them stir. They made a pattern in the rocks of turquoise and of green among the dark clusters of the mussels that hung everywhere like grapes. Dad would like some of the larger ones for fish bait. Thinking tenderly of him, Minna dropped a dozen into the sack she had remembered to bring with her. She was collecting, too, the tiniest shells of the abalone that tossed about the tide pools in all the colors of the rainbow; she could sell sets of them to little girls who loved them for their doll's dishes.

The sea anemones, too, were collectors of miniature shells, holding them with their sticky tentacles, perhaps as a sort of disguise. Those tentacles could suddenly burst into full bloom like the most extraordinary of chrysanthemums. And, if you were thinking in terms of a garden now, one could find asters, too. These were the sea urchins, of deep, rich crimson and purple color, each in the niche which it had carved with its endlessly working spines.

There was no end to the lure of the tide pools, at least as far as Minna was concerned, and she only regretted that she could not explore them all. She could never visit, either, all the grottoes and the caves to which the low tide had opened doors that soon would close again. One never knew what might be found in them, what spells of wondrous beauty might enthrall. . . .

Sitting beneath an arch of rocks tinted the most delicate shade of pinkish mauve and studded with the orange of the starfish, Minna fancied that she was in a mermaid's palace. And she herself was the mermaid, trailing a silvery tail among the feathery fronds of pink and coral seaweed.

It was here that she could forget about the Carnival, the humiliation of being asked to be a Grunion again, forget the dull routine of high school, forget about simply everything except the murmur of the sea. If she listened carefully, it might tell her secrets it had kept to itself since time began. She might be the reincarnated soul of a beautiful woman lost at sea and doomed forever to drift through its world-embracing waters, seeking the meaning of all things.

Half hypnotized by the sparkle of the water outside and its reflections upon the roof of the sea cave, Minna dreamed a mermaid's dreams. Her voice was witch music luring mariners to their doom; her hair was entwined with pearls. She was the Lorelei, combing her hair with a golden comb; she was the loveliest and most desirable of all creatures. She would never grow old and never die. . . .

Minna was rudely roused from her reverie by a wave that splashed in through the entrance and disturbed the crystal waters of the pool. Had she been her usual alert self, she would already have recognized the change in the sound of the sea. Echoing through the cavern, it now had a note of menace to any human so foolish as to be caught on the outermost reef. The tide was turning, and slowly and inexorably the great waters were sliding back to their own, back to cover, for another long while, the briefly disclosed magic of another world.

It was a world, too, of hungry mouths waiting for Mother Ocean to feed them. Abruptly, Minna Vail was no longer a mermaid princess but just a small girl in ragged tennis shoes and dripping blue jeans, who had not had her breakfast. Mother would be worrying about her now; and, as Minna thought of some of the chasms she would have to cross on the way back to shore, she was worried about herself.

It would be the laugh of the entire high school if Minnow Vail got trapped out on the rocks because she had daydreamed too long. Helicopter rescues were not uncommon along this coast, but they were reserved for tourists who didn't know any better. Tourists were expected to be landlubbers and consequently fools about the ocean. But it couldn't happen to a local girl! Minna could see herself pictured on the front page of the weekly newspaper, with the story, "Miss Minna Vail of 605 Holly Lane, Cliffside, explains her mishap by saying that she was dreaming about being a mermaid in a sea cave and didn't hear the tide coming in. Well-known leader of the Grunion troupe, Miss Vail may have been thinking of a promotion in her Carnival status. Big Mermaids often from little Grunions grow." End quote and ha-ha! The local reporter would have a field day, and so would her classmates. She would never hear the end of it; she would never be able to live it down.

And then the incredible happened, happened to her! What she had thought to be a mass of seaweed and flotsam moved a feeble wing—and, as she came closer, took the form of a great pelican, obviously almost dead from exhaustion, half-drowned. Somehow it had gotten itself all wound up in a fishing line. It lay between rocks, half caught, half floating—and altogether miserable. Probably it had been greedy, as most sea birds were, and had swallowed a hook. The way the bird was feebly struggling in its terror, she could not tell much except that it needed desperately to be freed. Tide or not, she could not leave it to die. She came closer, and dodging the pecks of its long and frantic beak, she rolled the large, queer-looking bird around and around. All the great creature did was to grunt and to struggle. Even under the very best of conditions it is hard to untangle a fish line. Usually one wound up by cutting it, but she had not brought her pocket knife. A barnacle or a razor-edged clam would have served, but none was at hand. In the end, she decided that the only possible course, with the waves swelling higher and higher in around them, was to carry the poor thing to shore.

With her sack under one arm, and the wriggling bird under the other, she made slow progress. The path around the rocks and through the tide pools was not an easy one at the best of times and, without the free use of her arms for balance, she kept slipping and almost fell on her face again and again. A person could easily break an arm, or an ankle or a leg, she thought. And with the crashing of the breakers and the thunder of the returning tide, who would hear her if she screamed? It was, as her mother was always telling her, a very hazardous thing to make a tide-pool expedition all alone. She would be due for a scolding—if and when she made it back to safety!

On the beach, tiny at first under the towering cliffs, she could see a figure watching her. As she came closer and it grew larger, she could hope against hope that it was Dad. Yes!

"A bit early to bring home a Thanksgiving turkey, isn't it?" was all he said as she wearily deposited her whole load upon the dry, firm sand. "Looks like a tough old bird, too!" Thank heavens, he was making jokes about it. If he was angry, as well he had a right to be, he would save it for later, perhaps after breakfast. Father was here now, and he was smiling, and that was most important.

"I went out to get you some mussels for bait, and see what I caught!"

But Father was already down on his knees, slashing the tangling line with his knife. The Gordian knot was "untied," as in the fable. The pelican was free. As it stretched its wings, they could see with relief that neither one was broken, nor the legs either. It even managed to stand. Then, solemn as an old man, the bird waddled away from them, looking a little apprehensively over its shoulder as if it still couldn't believe they were friendly. Then it seemed to regain its strength; it broke into a comic, lumbering run, spread wings that stretched wider than a man is tall, and suddenly was airborne in beautiful, graceful flight.

"Oh!" cried Minna, in wonder and relief.

"So that is that." Her father busied himself in setting up his long surf rod in its spike driven into the sand, accepted her mussels, and after splitting one open, put the bait onto a number six hook. "I told your mother I was going fishing this morning," he said, with a look at Minna that was warmer than any words could have been. "Now that you're back, I really will fish. No need to alarm her—I knew you'd be all right."

"That's the kind of father I've got!" Minna whispered proudly to herself as she ran up the steps toward home.

6

Minna's Triumph

Everyone had something exciting to talk about, it seemed, when the girls gathered for lunch Monday at their favorite, bird-decorated table under the eucalyptus trees. Today even the peanut butter and jelly sandwiches did not seem as tiresome as they had, especially since Betsy had brought along some crisp celery sticks which she loyally shared, and Laura donated thick slices of devil's food cake an inch deep in frosting. Separated for the whole weekend, they were in the mood for a tea party, and conversation bubbled.

Betsy and her family and their house guests had gone down to San Diego to visit the zoo that was famous all over the world (and developed by a woman, too!) and something to be remembered. "It's a botanical garden as well as a zoological one," Betsy said, quoting from the guide book and sounding very impressive. Then she lapsed into language to which she was more accustomed, composed of breathless phrases.

It was big—so big that you had to ride around it on a sort of bus to see everything, and then you could walk back to visit your special animals. The zoo was spread out over many narrow canyons; and everyone went from the top to the bottom of it and back again by moving stairways, which had been tremendous fun. She had walked through a tropical rain forest with all the bright-colored birds flying overhead, and she had seen the koala bears in another enclosure wrestling happily at the very tops of some big trees.

"They were so cute! Looked just like Teddy bears!" Minna had the feeling that Betsy regretted she had not been able to bring one of them home with her.

It was Laura who had the most enviable news to report. First thing on Friday night—after she and her family had gone to Palm Springs to visit an aunt who lived winters in a luxury resort in the desert—she had actually had a *date!* Friends had arranged it, and she had worn her powder-blue dress. "The one that floats," she explained, as though her friends were not already familiar with her wardrobe.

"A blind date, but boy-oh-boy, the minute I laid eyes on him—" Laura's cheeks were flushed and her brown eyes shone. With her curly dark hair, she was an unusually attractive girl, despite her tendency to be overweight, and could pass for years older than she really was.

"And what about when he looked at *you?*" Minna

wanted to know all the details. None of the girls had ever had what one might call an honest-to-goodness date, and they were hanging on Laura's words.

"The same! I—I think he has a crush." Laura obviously was still too thrilled about it all to act modest, but the other girls didn't mind. Given the same opportunity, they would have acted the same way. His name, it appeared, was Peter Stanley, and he went to a military school. He was tall, and he was gorgeous, and on Saturday night he had brought her an orchid.

"Of course, his mother raises them," Laura added, so as not to make too much of a good thing. Even with close friends, the story had to be reasonably believable.

"*Saturday* night, too?" Minna was slightly incredulous.

"Oh, yes! We spent most of Saturday together—he has a pool, and we swam. And then there was another party."

What had they talked about? Wasn't it hard, with a stranger and all?

"He wasn't a stranger for very long." Laura let them make the most of that remark before she added, "But he didn't try to kiss me the first night. I wouldn't have liked it, you know."

Her friends nodded in solemn agreement. Boys would think you were easy if you let them kiss you on the first date—all the girls' magazines said so. As for themselves, from their own experience, they wouldn't know.

"And on the second—on Saturday night?" Minna asked the question for the other two.

"Well, we went out on the terrace and danced under

the stars—they're so big and bright in the desert—and. . . ." Laura suggested what she could not bring herself to put into words. A boy had kissed her, and it had been like an electric shock!

"And what were you wearing Saturday night?" Ciss struck a realistic note.

"Well, I had my white sunback with me, but my aunt didn't like it. Said it was too girlish and simple. She—she—" and again Laura paused meaningfully, "she had a black sheath that just happened to fit me."

Now that she had gone this far, had admitted that she had worn the black that every girl desired but often at fifteen was not permitted by conservative parents, Laura would give them a complete description of her outfit. Black, with rhinestone jewelry, and to cap it all, her aunt's mink stole!

Minna looked with scorn at her old cardigan and the plaid skirt that needed pressing, quite ignoring the fact that Laura today was dressed in similar fashion. She was frankly envious. Laura had met a boy from military school; one who must be nothing at all like the clods they saw all around them every day at Cliffside High—a boy, tall and straight in his uniform—not pudgy, square, and sloppy, like Bob Jones for instance. And she had danced with him under the stars of a desert night, wearing a black sheath with rhinestone jewelry and dragging real mink! In fashion ads, women always dragged their mink.

A person had to go away from home to meet somebody

interesting. There was nobody in Cliffside High who compared with the glowing description that Laura had given of Peter Stanley. In Cliffside there were no romantic desert nights, no dancing to speak of except on Friday afternoons in the school gymnasium. Unless somebody asked you to the prom, which for a sophomore girl was as unlikely as a zebra changing its stripes to polka dots.

Minna was still cross at Bob Jones for not letting her use his surfboard and for ignoring her that day on the beach. If she were one of those girls who sat around posing and looking pretty and afraid to get their hair wet—or a silly giggler like that girl from Latin class he seemed to admire so much—he and his gang might take a different view of her.

But where would be the fun in all that? They were such ordinary boys! And besides, you couldn't pretend you were something you weren't and miss hours of frolic in the ocean. She decided that she would have to find another way for herself, but what could it possibly be?

She was enjoying being cold and indifferent to Bob Jones, and making a point of not once glancing at him during geometry class or afterward in the hall. She could do the assignments by herself—thank you very much!—and she didn't need a mite of help from Bob Jones or anybody.

"What's the matter, Minna?" He had tried to stop her one day as she was hurrying to catch up with Hans Van Der Oster.

"Figure it out for yourself!" She had tossed her head in

what she hoped was a spirited gesture. "If you don't know, I can't tell you." And she ran on in the general direction of Hans.

Mother had taken a fancy to the Dutch boy, and with help from Father she was trying to make him feel at home in America. She had found some of Minna's brother Hugh's outgrown jeans and cords and sweat shirts for Hans to wear, and he was looking less and less strange and more like a typical high school student.

Hans, in his turn, was doting on Mother, and as the weeks passed he was spending more of his spare hours at the Vail home than at the Schmidts'. It was none of Bob's business to know it was Mother, and not Minna herself, who was the main attraction for Hans. Mother—and Mother's cooking.

"I like to see a boy eat," she said, again and again filling his plate, and stocking the cooky jar for him. She and Dad missed Hugh, missed him more lately than they had mentioned, and Minna sensed that they welcomed Hans as a substitute son. "In America, men help with the housework," Mother explained, asking Hans to peel potatoes and set the table. He had been so puzzled the first time that it had been laughable.

"You see, most of us don't have servants as you probably have in Amsterdam." Mother was tactful but also firm. "Women work outside the home at all sorts of jobs nowadays, and they can't be expected to do everything at home, too!"

Hans was a bright boy, and his English was improving

rapidly. If people talked to him slowly enough and didn't use slang, he could understand almost everything that was said to him. And how he could tango! Yet this was only the beginning of his accomplishments in the field of ballroom dancing. He also could do the samba and the rhumba, he could soft-shoe and tap.

"My father died in a Nazi concentration camp." Hans was matter-of-fact about the tragedy that came as only one of many in the crushing of his country by the German hordes. "We were much at home, and we were a very close-knit family. My older sisters needed me as a partner, and they have taught me."

He was giving a picture of the Hollanders that was far from the conventional idea of fat burghers and stolid women in elaborate costumes and wooden shoes. One got the wrong ideas about other countries if one had never visited them and knew none of its people. Probably there wasn't so much as a windmill any more in all of Holland, and not so much as one tulip! Minna felt better when Hans assured her that they still had plenty of both, as she simply couldn't visualize Holland without them.

As for Hans, his own ideas about America had been equally limited, having got most of them from the movies. All Americans were rich and owned two or three cars and never wore the same clothes twice. They lived among cowboys and Indians and gunfighting gangsters. . . .

Minna was keeping her practice sessions of dancing with Hans a secret, even from her closest friends. She was waiting for a time when she could startle them; meanwhile, she was enjoying herself.

"You are not so bad, my friend." Occasionally Hans gave her a rare compliment, too, but he was not adept at what in America was called "soft soap." He was hard on Minna, brutally critical for the most part. They were not ready—or she at least was not ready—to do the tango in the high school gym on a Friday afternoon. "Do you think I want to make a fool of myself?"

"Maybe you don't, but I do!" Minna was, for once, insistent. "They won't know the difference, honestly! We can just sort of go through the motions." Minna could not wait to see everybody's expressions. The girls would be dancing together, the boys probably just milling around, and only a few couples would be brave enough to actually dance with each other. "I'm going to bring the tango record Friday, and I'm expecting you to be there!"

On this special Friday afternoon, she wore her fullest skirt so that she could swoop and sway. It was an old skirt, but she was tired of her tight ones, she said, as she and her friends trooped up to the gymnasium. Nobody really liked the Friday afternoon dances, but everyone went full of hope that *this* Friday it would be different. The school called it "socializing," but it never went off very successfully.

Minna made sure that Bob Jones was there before she put on her record and then held out her arms to Hans. Bob was stupefied, and so were the rest of them. She and Hans had the floor all to themselves, and Minna for one made the very most of it. Even Hans whispered in her ear that today she was *gut*.

The finish was her departure on a note of triumph and upon the arm of Hans. Thank goodness his old-world gallantry had sustained him to the last, especially with the promise of chocolate pudding later. Minna could take a package mix and fix it herself.

And soon her phone was ringing. Laura was incredulous, Betsy outraged that she had not been told, and Ciss—as always—realistic. "Good show," Ciss said. "Congratulations, Minnow. You pulled a fast one on us."

And then there was a boy's voice over the phone, high-pitched at first and then low. It must be embarrassing to be a boy whose voice was changing and who had to identify himself with a squeak. "Bob," he said. "Bob Jones!" he managed somehow. "How—how would you like to go to the movies tonight if you haven't anything better to do, huh?"

"It's awfully nice of you to ask me, Bob. But—" Minna hesitated, trying to remember what you were supposed to do when a boy asked you for a date at the last minute. She had read somewhere that one must be pleasant about it, but not act too eager. "I'm awfully sorry, but I—I'm busy."

Well, she *was* busy. She had planned to go over to see her grandmother.

"Maybe skin diving tomorrow, then? We haven't gone for a heck of a long time."

That was his fault and not hers, but Minna did not

choose to remind him. Instead she decided that this was the time to act like one of those girls on the beach who had to be coddled. "It's pretty cold still, and I'll freeze!"

"Don't give me that!" Bob sounded puzzled. "Not with a rubber suit on, you won't."

"But mine has a leak in it, Bob. Don't you remember? I snagged myself on a rock, and I don't know how in the world to fix it . . . " her voice trailed off helplessly.

Minna knew that she had scored when she heard Bob snort. What kind of a girl had she turned into when she couldn't take care of her own repairs? When a boy had to come over and do them for her? But he accepted the new state of affairs.

"Thank you, Bob," she finished, her voice as sugary as she could make it. "I'll be looking for you, then. Right after lunch."

Minna hung up, feeling rather smug about the whole thing. Men weren't so difficult to handle when you went about it the right way. And Bob, for all his shortcomings, was excellent material to get in a little practice on.

7

Another World

"Well, Minnow—for heaven's sweet sake, aren't you going to carry *anything?*" Bob was already loaded down with the two rubber suitpacks and two heavy pairs of flippers when Minna handed him the crowbars and the weights.

"Of course," she said airily as she swung two face masks from one arm and picked up the inner tube with the other. "I guess that's all. What do you say—let's go!"

"Say, what's got into you, Minnow?" Bob grumbled all the way down to the beach.

"Don't you wish you knew?" Minna skipped on ahead, leading the way down the steep path, Bob following close behind and in danger every single minute of falling headlong with his load of paraphernalia. "You're big and strong, aren't you?" she said teasingly when he paused for a moment's rest. "At least that's what I've heard some of the other girls say."

"Name one!" Bob was getting crosser by the minute. "Honestly, Minnow! You used to be such a good sport, a regular pal, like one of the fellows!"

"That was my mistake. . . ." But Minnow said it under her breath. She was wondering how far she could go before Bob actually exploded. Something told her to ease off a little. She was really eager to go skin diving today, and if she pressed her advantage beyond limits, Bob might easily give up the whole project and go home in a huff. You never went skin diving alone, but always with a "buddy" in case something happened. Bob was such a powerful swimmer that a girl felt perfectly safe with him along—much safer than with some of the others who sometimes had to be rescued themselves when they got tangled in the kelp.

She was rubbing seaweed over the glass of his face mask when he finally groaned and grunted his way across the beach and dropped his load beside her. "Fixing yours first, Bob," she said, smiling up at him with a tender, innocent expression. "I'm going to do such a good job that it won't fog over the way it did last time."

"Glad you're still good for *something,*" he answered ungraciously, as he listened to the thunder of the surf with an appraising ear. They were in an isolated cove where few skin divers came except on days when it was calm, and now the beat and thunder of the waves made both of them pause. The tide was churning over the rocks and beating against the cliffs with a force so great that anyone who knew the ocean would think twice about defying it. They would have to wait for a lull, and that might take the rest of the afternoon if it came at all.

"You're a funny person, do you know that, Minnow?" Bob was lolling against the sun-warmed rocks. "Sometimes you act like a girl—like when you did the tango with Dutchy—and then sometimes I almost forget you're not a boy."

"Well, I'm a girl all right, and don't you forget it!" Minna threatened him with a handful of sand. "And what's more, this year at the Carnival I'm going to be a Mermaid!" She threw her head back and laughed so that he would not take her too seriously. "Only don't tell anybody. Don't you think it's about time, though?" She was anxiously watching his reaction.

"Who's kidding who? Yah—I'm going to be the Octopus! Will you vote for me?"

Minna was secretly relieved that Bob thought she was only kidding, since his response had been so rude, refusing to take her seriously. It would be awful if he told his whole gang of her ambition and they started tormenting her by singing that old song about "Minnie the Mermaid" whenever she came by.

"Oh, sure—I'll stuff the ballot box. You're the most popular boy in town, and everyone concedes it." Minna continued her banter in a lighthearted vein. The role of Octopus was the most coveted one in the entire pageant, and no one ever knew who it was to be until the very last moment. It was the Octopus who would rule as Carnival

King Neptune for the festivities the following year—and he had to choose some girl to be his Queen.

"Oh, the heck with the old Carnival! Guess we'll both have to stick to the ocean, eh, Minnow?" Bob rolled over on his arms and stretched his length to the sun, as though that settled the entire matter. He was just about as romantic as—Minna reached for some invidious comparison—as a *sand-fly*. And he would grow up to have a fat wife and seven children with runny noses. She could not imagine ever letting him kiss her, but one had to be in a special mood for that, she guessed. Yet a girl couldn't help wondering what it would be like to be kissed, and whether you fell in love with the boy afterwards or not.

Some girls had been kissed and some hadn't. But either way, one did not have to act like an absolute goose—like Laura. Ever since that trip of hers to Palm Springs, Laura had been floating around on cloud nine, and the whole crowd was getting disgusted with her. Whenever she had a letter from that boy, she carried it around with her and read it at frequent intervals, always making a point of showing that the envelope had a special delivery stamp on it.

In the years since Minna had known Laura, they had had tiffs from time to time but always had made them up within a few days' time. They had been best friends since they were in third grade. But how could you stay best friends now with a girl who, when you phoned her, gave a long, disappointed sigh and said, "Oh, it's only *you!* I was sorta hoping it was long distance."

As for Laura, she had been cross last night at Minna for not having told her that she was learning the tango, that she had kept it as a surprise. The two girls had never before come near to being at sword-point, but now. . . . Mother said it was only a phase. Evidently she regarded it to be as simple as a case of the mumps or the measles, from which they would inevitably recover.

In spite of herself, Minna had to admit that it was rather fun being here on the beach with Bob, and for the time being at least she put the quarrel with Laura out of her mind. She fell to building sand castles to while away the time, and he enthusiastically joined her. Laura—there she popped up again—would consider this merely child's play.

As always, the Pacific had a calming influence upon Minna, and how she loved what she privately called "her ocean," in all its everchanging moods. And so often it was far from what might be called "Pacific." In this mightiest of oceans, the waters swept unobstructed for thousands upon thousands of miles until they lashed this shore. With absolutely nothing in between—except Catalina out there on the horizon.

It was several hours before the waves gentled down, and then other skin divers joined them as by unspoken signal. There was a group of boys about Bob's age, one other girl, and several older men with oxygen tanks. Scuba diving with the big tanks let you go down to considerable depths and stay under for a long time, but it was dangerous unless you had considerable experience in it. An alarming number of foolhardy amateurs had lost their lives; and Bob's folks, like Minna's parents, had put down an absolute veto. You had to take lessons and learn the fundamentals in a swimming pool; Bob and Minna both were deeply envious of anyone who could really "dive scuba."

Each of them would always remember the great thrill it had been when they first acquired the rubber suits that at least marked them a step above the ordinary swimmers. The suits had been expensive, too; it had taken hours of grass cutting, starfish peddling, and firewood gathering to acquire the money to buy them. Also some persuasion of parents to help out. Until you had a rubber suit, you were nothing but a summer swimmer, little better than a *tourist!* That word, to a youthful resident of Cliffside, was anathema.

By this time Minna's suit had so many patches on it that she often compared herself with Raggedy Ann. The suits were somewhat delicate, and you had to put them on carefully, almost like nylons, or they would tear. After adjusting the weights about her waist along with a knife, Minna followed Bob down to the edge of the surf. They would have to swim out between *frames,* the bigger waves that could tumble them over and over, especially with flippers on. They were terribly awkward in flippers on land or in shallow water, and had to waddle like pelicans.

Yet part of the excitement was this challenge at the edge of the sea. If their timing was right, they could seize the moment and then make it out to calmer water beyond the breakers before a wave could grab hold of them. . . .

Bob was the first to go out, pushing the inner tube ahead of him that—with a gunny sack suspended beneath it—would hold their catch, if any. And Minna followed as closely behind him as the movement of Bob's churning feet would permit. The seas were still running so high at moments that she wanted to stay near to a friend. "Not afraid of these little ripples, are you, Minnow?" Bob faced her, treading water.

"Wouldn't be here if I were, would I?" Minna grasped the rubber raft and began adjusting the snorkel tube attached to her face mask. She and Bob had agreed that today they'd try a new hunting ground; and now, cruising face down above the transparent depths, Minna was watching for an outcropping of submarine rocks that might yield them rich picking of abalones. With the snorkel, she need not lift her head to breathe. . . .

Though she had seen all this many times before, the wonders of the underwater world were always new and intriguing; it was a mystic place, and you could speculate on what might be hidden among these shadowy, glimmering valleys and gardens where the silver schools of fish were at home and a human being was an utter stranger, an alien. The unknown always tempted one—but you had to conquer fear to explore it, to take the first dive down into the depths.

Bob was already swimming easily down there, but without much luck in booty as far as she could see. Distances were hard to judge under water, and apparently he was finding that he could not reach bottom here. They never went below twenty or at most thirty feet; you risked breaking your eardrums if you tried that, and ran out of breath, and had to come up to the surface too fast. They would have to move on to a shallower reef.

"Are you going to stay up here all day like one of those glass-bottomed boats?" Bob surfaced beside her and breathed deeply in and out, preparing for his second plunge.

"What's the particular rush?" Minna was enjoying watching the undulations of a strand of kelp that rose almost to the surface from its hold on the ocean's floor, swaying gently to and fro like trees in the wind. It framed an undersea world of muted pinks and blues and greens; there were lanes and corridors leading on into the fathomless abyss. With one kick of her fins she could travel down, could go anywhere she liked above the ever-changing terrain, here a weed or moss-covered rock she could reach out and touch, there a ledge or cliff that promised abalone. She was living in another dimension.

Now for it. She took a last gulp of air and headed downward. Propelled with the effortless ease of the swim fins, she had the strange sensation of being a bird that was able to fly without using its wings. She was gliding through a quiet dream world, moving like an apparition beneath the bright ceiling overhead, but limited by the precious seconds she could hold her breath under the sea's pressure. If she moved slowly, she could hold it for well over a minute, which in these alien surroundings was a minute suspended in time.

She found a big overhanging crevice of rock, and had seen enough to convince her that she had discovered abalone which were big enough to take. If a person was caught with any little ones in his possession he would have to pay a serious fine; but if they were large enough the meat could be pounded into delicious steaks for the table at home, or they could be sold to the fish market in town. The rough shells of the abalone, covered with barnacles and sea weed so that they resembled rocks, were simply beautiful inside, each one different but each iridescent with all the colors of a peacock's tail. These shells, too, could be sold, sometimes. Both she and Bob, like most of the younger set at Cliffside, had an eye out for business and for extra cash. Bounty from the sea. . . .

Bob had brought up two spiny lobsters—the Pacific coast kind that were actually giant crayfish and had almost no claws—and he was smug about his catch when she returned to the surface empty-handed. But not for long. She needed one of the small crowbars to pry the abalone loose from their powerful suction grip on the rocks far below among the nooks and crannies.

He followed her down to see for himself, carrying a fish spear in case he might sight some more sporting quarry than these motionless mollusks. And it was Bob who sighted the reptilian head of the vicious moray lurking in its hole. . . .

In her eagerness to pry loose her first prize, an abalone

as big as a soup plate, she had thrust her hands into one of the crevices without checking to see what else might be lurking there. And now, as Bob made the thrust with his spear, she was looking straight into the evil eyes, the wide-open mouth packed with needle-sharp teeth that could pierce a finger to the bone.

Fortunately Bob made a direct hit on the big eel, transfixing the green monster before it could strike. He took it, wriggling and snapping still, up to the surface. They would now have an exciting adventure to report instead of a painful casualty; but the shock of horror remained for both of them as they looked at the stubby, thick-bodied creature squirming in the sack. Minna hated to seem chicken and suggest that she had enough of diving for the day. She would go down again if Bob suggested it, but she was grateful when he was the one to start the movement back to shore. And he hadn't even given her a scolding for going into the crevice without looking to see what was ahead of her.

8

Laura

Laura was not at school on Monday, which was not entirely unusual; she was a creature of moods and could always get her parents to write her the necessary note to present at the office when she came back. For some reason Minna did not call her friend that night. There had been a slight coolness between them ever since the afternoon when Minna had danced the tango with Hans.

Minna had missed Laura at lunch with the other girls under the eucalyptus tree, and missed her even more later when they usually walked home together, but she would not give her friend the satisfaction of knowing this. Let Laura call and make up. There had been bargains today in the windows of the little dress shops where they liked to linger after school to see what was new—and more important than that, what was on clearance. If Laura had been at her side to egg her on, Minna might have been tempted to ask one of the salesladies to put a certain sweater aside on one of the "layaway plans" that were always such an enticement. You paid a dollar down and then scrambled for the rest of the money. Without Laura beside her to help her decide between the pink and the blue, Minna was able to resist, though.

There was something about an old friend like Laura that had become part of Minna, and that she missed dreadfully. She remembered the nice things about Laura, things like last Christmastime when she had shared her glamorous lingerie with Minna who, as usual, had been gifted in this category only with tailored broadcloth pajamas and a "sensible" white slip. Laura's aunt in Palm Springs had sent her a whole matched set in "Green Siren" trimmed with "phantom lace," and Laura had insisted that she didn't like the baby-doll pajamas and that Minna must have them. Laura could be like that. She knew how Minna felt sometimes without her ever saying a word.

But now Minna was stubborn, and she just wouldn't call Laura. Let Laura call her first. The phone rang several times that evening, but it was always for Mother. For some reason which Minna could not have explained even to herself, she felt vaguely uneasy; she found it harder even than usual to study her homework.

Laura's phoning or not phoning was not that important, she tried to tell herself as several days passed with no word from her friend. Ciss and Betsy had not heard from her, either, which was strange.

"You'd think when a person has a phone right beside their bed they could let you know what was going on, wouldn't you? I mean if they had a cold or something," Ciss remarked.

"Maybe she's gone out of town, but I don't think so. I saw their car in the driveway," was Betsy's contribution.

They speculated idly all through lunch for several days. Cliffside wasn't so large a town that a person was apt to drop out of sight in it. Still, no one had answered the phone any of the times when Betsy and Ciss had tried to reach the Adamses. It was a sure-enough mystery and Minna slipped out of the house one night late in the week to try to solve it.

Laura and her family had recently moved into the hills above the town. As Minna wound her way upward along roads that intersected lanes which made a maze where it was hard to find one's way even by daylight, she regretted her rashness. After dark the dogs of Cliffside took on a new and menacing aspect, and rattling their chains or leaping against fences, dared any pedestrian to pass. According to the dogs, the only proper way to travel was by car.

The hillside was a spangle of lights from the houses along the various terraces, and far below where the highway rimmed the ocean, a stream of auto headlights moved in a shimmering band. Yet a girl's mind was not upon the view when she was expecting some fanged canine monster to break loose from his yard at any moment and leap on her. It was not that she was exactly afraid of strange dogs, Minna tried to tell herself, but she could do without them. Especially now.

Even householders living up here seemed to regard the crunch of footsteps on the gravel of the roadway with suspicion, and here and there she encountered the sudden glare of floodlights turned upon the porches and lawns to ward away intruders. And it was not as though it were the middle of the night or something; it was not yet nine o'clock.

Dad would have driven her, but he had gone to a lodge meeting and dropped Mother off at her bridge club. Somehow, too, Minna hated to voice to them her growing apprehension about Laura because they would laugh at her and say it was ridiculous. If a girl's parents chose to let her miss a whole week of school, that should be no concern of the Vails. One didn't stick his nose into other people's business—especially in Cliffside! While in population it rated as a small town, it had in many respects the aspects of a much larger city. People had come here from many parts of the country; some were retiring after distinguished or successful careers, others to run the motels and restaurants that catered to the ever-changing throng of tourists. It was live and let live. Beatniks, artists, writers, conservative folk who devoted their whole time to gardening, aircraft engineers, retired opera singers, technicians and actors from Hollywood all called Cliffside home, but mingled only in the supermarkets.

As Minna trudged up the hill and glanced at various

names on the illuminated mail boxes, she became aware of many strangers, many new homes, and many, many dogs with chips on their shoulders. This was the new section of town, and almost no one knew anybody else. One did not think much about such things in the broad light of day, when tramping by boldly or more usually whisked along by automobile or bicycle. But it was no place for a lonely stroll after dark.

When at last she reached the Adams house, Minna was only slightly reassured by a small light burning in the upper story, if one could call it that. The house was cantilevered over a canyon, suspended on several different levels, and neither Minna nor Laura liked it as well as something a bit more old-fashioned and comfortable. It might be the last word in modern architecture but, as the girls said, one could scarcely tell the front from the back.

Now as Minna tripped over an array of hoses left like a tangle of dead snakes across the path, she grew irritated. The Adamses could at least pick them up when they were through watering the patio, and not leave them for somebody to trip over. No one had bothered to gather up the small rolls of advertising sheets or the throwaway advertising "newspapers" that boys were paid to deliver helter-skelter and that hardly anybody ever bothered to read. The entire place had an uncared-for look that was not at all what you would expect of the Adamses. Minna decided to ring the bell only once and that faintly; then if no one answered she would creep quietly away.

It was Laura's father who flung the door wide open, and with the dazed look of a man taken utterly by surprise, beckoned for her to come in. "Oh, yes—it's Minna Vail, isn't it?" No one else was in sight, not even Billy, Laura's younger brother, known as The Pest. Minna would at the moment have even welcomed the sight of Billy with his squirt gun, or the raucous sound of his cowboy-and-Indian shows on TV, in the midst of this silent house.

"You've come about Laura, I expect," Mr. Adams said, leading the way into the living room and switching on the lights. "Well, she has a serious case of polio—the bulbar type. We don't expect her to live, and even if she does—" Mr. Adams sank to the couch and hid his face in his hands.

Minna stared past him into the black space beyond the picture window, seeing nothing. Everything was blank; she was unable to comprehend. "Oh!" she whispered.

He went on, in a voice that was old and tired. Laura was up in Los Angeles at the Cedars of Lebanon Hospital and her mother was with her. But the specialists there offered very little in the way of hope.

"But didn't she—didn't she have her shots?"

Mr. Adams raised his head, and his hollow eyes sought Minna's. "The Salk vaccine? Well, you know Laura. She dreaded being stuck in the arm, and her mother and I didn't insist on it as we should have, so we kept postponing it. I can never forgive myself. . . ."

He had the white, drawn, disheveled look of a man who has neither eaten nor slept for days. "It's good of you to come," he said, with politeness that was obviously difficult. "I—I didn't think I wanted to see anyone, but now that you're here, it's good to talk to you. It's good to talk to anyone besides myself . . . . "

It can't seem real to him yet, Minna thought. It isn't real to me! Laura, plump and pretty Laura, would come running into the living room in a minute to pick up the sweater she had been knitting and which she had left on one of the chairs. Laura would turn on the hi-fi . . . Laura would appear with her hair done in curlers and say this was a *fine* time of night for anyone to come calling. Laura would pirouette before the glass and say that she hadn't lost a pound, but didn't it look as though she had? Laura. . . .

"I—I hope it isn't as bad as you think, Mr. Adams." Minna was trying to recall what her mother might say at a time like this by way of consolation. "Sometimes, you know, with all these miracle drugs. . . ." Her voice trailed away, lacking any ring of conviction. Under these circumstances, Mother would think of something to do to help, some positive action to take. Maybe not about Laura, but certainly for Laura's father. "Whatever's wrong, a bit of food will usually come in handy. People have to eat!" she would always say as she carried a casserole or some soup or chicken to a home where there was sickness or trouble.

"I'm going to fix you something to eat, Mr. Adams! I

bet you haven't eaten properly in days." Minna leaped to her feet, glad of a chance for some activity. She thought —surely there must be bacon in the refrigerator, and eggs. The simple, everyday things she could handle. . . . "If you don't eat what I cook, I'll never never speak to you again," she said, trying to force a feeble note of gaiety. No matter what was happening up in Los Angeles, this poor man needed somebody to take care of him now. He needed bacon and eggs and hot toast and marmalade and the strongest coffee she could brew.

"You've always meant so much to Laura, I know." He stood in the doorway as Minna busied herself about the kitchen, trying to find what she needed in a strange place. At home she could have laid her hands on anything instantly, even in the dark.

"I can't say much for your housekeeping, Mr. Adams." The place really was a mess, with oddments of food here and there, milk left on the sink to sour, dirty coffee cups and dirty dishes and coffee grounds like brown snow in the sink.

"I drove my wife and Laura up to the city," he said, as though that explained it. But after all, they must have left in frantic haste. "We thought at first she had only one of those virus cold things that are always going around. And then—" He shook his head. "I only got back tonight, because there was nothing I could do up at the hospital. Dropped Billy off at his aunt's place. Forgot his underwear and his play shoes and everything," he added.

"Like 'em sunny side up?" Minna asked as finally she

got eggs sizzling in one pan and bacon in the other. Her knowledge of cookery went little beyond the bacon-and-egg stage, but this she had mastered—and she knew that her father always said eggs should be cooked in butter and not in the bacon grease. Anyway, this way if you were lucky, you got them both done at the same time.

"I didn't know it, but I guess I was hungry." Mr. Adams sniffed at the good smell of coffee now permeating the room, and went to set the table. He had perked up a little bit. "You know, you're just what the doctor ordered, Minna."

Once Minna had him served and eating, she plunged up to the elbows in dish water, glad to have the simple homely task of cleaning up the kitchen to distract her thoughts from Laura. She didn't want to break down and cry in front of Mr. Adams, so she turned on the radio above the sink and let in a cheerful blast of music.

"Anything else I can get for you?" she called to Mr. Adams, and not waiting for his answer brought in more toast and refilled his coffee cup. "I'm going to run on pretty soon, or Mother and Dad will be getting worried about me."

"You didn't walk all the way up here, did you? By yourself, in the dark?"

"No, I came by dog sled!" She again tried to make a feeble joke. "I'll just call Dad, and he'll run up and get me." As she picked up the phone, another thought occurred to her. She hated to leave poor Mr. Adams alone. The wind had begun to rise and was singing like a muffled, mournful voice in the chimney. They must be going to have a storm, which was all this lonely, stricken, hilltop place needed. Wouldn't it be of some comfort to him to come down and spend the night with the Vails? They had plenty of room for him with Hugh away, and Mother would be quick to ask him if she knew. Mother would want him to stay as long as he liked if it would be any consolation to him to have other people around. She drew a big breath and asked him.

Mr. Vail shook his head. He couldn't leave the phone —he was expecting a call from the hospital at any hour of the day or night. But he would let Minna know, he promised. He'd phone her the news, good or bad.

They were in the hallway now, and inadvertently Minna's eyes had turned to the open door of Laura's room. There in the middle of the rug was a pair of woolly slippers which had been kicked aside. She caught, too, a whiff of the spicy carnation cologne which Laura always used, and it was suddenly all too much for Minna.

She had tried to be brave and grown-up for Mr. Adams' sake, tried to act as her mother would have done in such an emergency, but now she collapsed, blubbering, "She'll b-be back, Mr. Adams, you wait and s-s-see!" Her face worked in anguish, and she buried it in her arms, shoulders shaking. She had gone beyond her depth.

"There, there, child." He stroked her head gently and picked up the phone. "I'll get your father here on the double."

Minna was lost in wonder and grief. It was only *old*

people who died, after they had lived out their lives. Not one of your friends, not a girl who had been close to you since you were both in pigtails and pinafores! The tears were streaming down Minna's cheeks like the rain on the windshield as she leaned against her father's shoulder in the car on the way down the hill.

"Wonderful rain!" Her father seized upon the weather as a topic to distract her. "A good rain always does wonders for Southern California, and there's been precious little of it so far this year." His conversation rambled on, the mere sound of it a comfort. What he said didn't matter; there was nothing for anyone to say, nothing that mattered really at all.

Mother was waiting to greet her with a cup of cocoa, with the sound of the water running into the tub for Minna's bath. "My poor lamb." Mother put her arms around Minna, whose tears welled up afresh.

The worst part of it was that she and Laura had not parted as friends. She had been jealous of Laura in the last few weeks whenever they had seen each other. Minna had said mean things about her, had been just as horrid as one girl could be to another. And now Laura was going to die, and she would never have a chance to make it up to her.

"Perhaps you will, dear," Mother tried to console her. Laura had youth on her side, and might pull through this. Miracles had happened. "And remember there are some worse things than death, dear. Laura might be a hopeless cripple if she lived. Now try to get some sleep. . . ." Mother sat beside the bed, with Minna's hand tight in hers. "We must think about what is best for Laura, and all we can do now is to leave her in God's hands."

9

Dear Cousin

Laura had shown a slight improvement, Mr. Adams said, calling next morning when they were still at the breakfast table. Thank God—he had used the familiar phrase as a prayer, and all the Vails echoed it. The sun sparkled; the soft air through the open window of the dining room was fresh with the smell of rain-washed flowers. Roses, English violets, the first of the jasmine—one could gather a bouquet from the smell of the air.

"This is the day that the Lord has made. Let us rejoice and be glad in it." Minna looked at her father who had, unexpectedly, given voice to Biblical expression. He was not a religious man, and he seldom went to church. But you did not have to go to church to pray, Minna realized.

"Our Father," Mother began, rising from her chair. One never knew how parents felt, or would react. Never knew how close their hearts were to their children's. . . .

Today was the first of Minna's Easter vacation; and now, as her father suggested, she might dare to be glad in it. It wouldn't do the slightest bit of good to stay around the house moping and worrying about Laura, and Mother had a sensible solution. She needed Minna's aid in her gift shop "to keep an eye on the Easter bunnies."

Bunnies to any dweller of Cliffside were not the darling pink-eyed kind that went around eating carrots and distributing baskets. They were boys and girls from high schools and colleges inland who invaded Cliffside and other towns along the coast for their annual springtime frolic. And, while they were there, did not care how they acted. They were reckless and gay and usually abominable.

Cliffside loathed the Easter bunnies. They shoplifted . . . they had rowdy beach parties . . . they drove the police crazy . . . and finally departing, some left behind dreadful messes.

Cliffside braced itself for the traditional Easter bunny invasion as, in other sections of the country, one might prepare for a hurricane. No one welcomed them except greedy landlords who could charge exorbitant rents for a week or two and did not care who broke up the tawdry sticks of beach furniture . . . who did not care what went on at these poorly chaperoned house parties. As Minna's father said, landlords like this should be "strung up," but never were.

So, in her own fashion, Minna faced Easter bunny week. She had been too young to be much bothered by it in earlier years, but now she had to admit that these barefooted contemporaries of hers were a mess. They wandered about in hordes. As she saw them day after day in her mother's shop, they were unspeakably rude, and some of them were thieves. They had to be watched every minute or they would walk out—almost with the cash register. If they were caught in the act, they said they were doing it "for kicks." Taken as a whole, there was nothing cute about them—or about her cousin Lucia.

The Vails didn't even know that she was in Cliffside until she stopped outside of the house with a male contingent and nonchalantly descended from a car driven by one of her swains. "I'm supposed to report in here," Lucia said with an affected drawl she had acquired since Minna had last seen her. "Mother and Dad think I am staying with you down here, and I thought you ought to know."

The accompanying males tittered, and Mr. Vail reddened with anger. It was Mother who invited them in to sit around the fire while she prepared cocoa for the crowd. "We've plenty of room for you here, my dear," Mother said. "You know you're always welcome."

How could Mother be polite when Lucia was acting so badly, when she was condescendingly referring to their house as "part of that old Cliffside charm you hear so much about." She was a blonde now instead of a redhead, and her lashes were dripping with mascara. If looks could kill, Minna's would have as Lucia and her circle gathered around to enjoy the fire kindled with the wood Minna had so laboriously dragged up from the beach.

A person did not do that to the Vails, did not invade with a lot of strange boys, not bother to introduce them, and yet expect to be entertained. These were dreadful boys—as Minna viewed them—white and thin and gulping their cocoa. Instead of conquests to boast about, Lucia seemed to have swept the alleys for the lonely and unwanted. And yet she had an air. Lucia always had an air. Wherever she was, she claimed—and held—the center of attention.

"Dear cousin," she gushed over Minna and drew her unwillingly into an embrace.

"So we're relatives. So what?" Minna freed herself and wished Lucia would stop prattling about how Minna was the best little swimmer you ever saw—a regular daredevil, you know. That's why they call her "Minnow." Did you ever meet a girl named Minnow before? And she has the cutest act in the Carnival every summer. She's a Grunion, and wouldn't that kill you?

"I thought they were a myth," one of the boys who had sorted himself out as Harold spoke up. "But now I see they're a *Miss.*"

The crowd laughed, and Minna flushed with embarrassment. The talk was too fast for her, and she could not think of a comeback. She could not think of anything to say except that the real grunions would be running on several nights at the end of the week.

"Oh, good, let's have a beach party, and you can show us some, darling."

"That will be up to the grunions," Minna muttered, wishing she could think of some way to refuse her cousin's invitation.

When Lucia finally departed in a whiff of perfume that lingered (was it *My Sin* or *Temptation?*) Minna and her father held a council of war. Minna wouldn't go to the beach party, and her father was ready to call Lucia's parents and tell them to come down and get her. She was his own brother's daughter, and he needed to be told plenty.

"Do as you like, dear," Mother was the only calm one, "but I don't think it will do any good. You can't take a girl her age and give her a spanking. In my opinion, the best thing will be to try to keep an eye on Lucia and see that she doesn't come to any harm."

Most of these youngsters who came down here were only kicking up their heels and showing off, Mother pointed out, and it was only a comparative few who caused the real trouble and gave all the Easter bunnies a bad name. Still there was danger, particularly at night in sheltered coves, and Mother insisted that Minna go to the beach party. With Minna on hand, Lucia would have to watch her step. "She knows that Minna will tell."

So now Minna was supposed to be a chaperone. Minna would call Laura who would die laughing—it was her first reaction. Sadly, she remembered that she couldn't.

"And anyway, dear, maybe you will catch some grunions. It has been done, you know, and I love them for breakfast."

On the night of the beach party, Minna grumbled her way into her heaviest sweat shirt and the most ragged of her jeans. If she were going to catch grunions, she couldn't dress like a pantywaist. At times she might be up to her waist in the ocean. If the grunions came at all, the slim, tiny, delectable fish were quick, and they were tricky. There couldn't be any fooling around with grunions, not wanting to get wet. And it would be cold on the beach. The grunions came only on certain tides, and tonight's was set for ten o'clock.

"Sounds as if they had an alarm clock in their heads," Lucia said, greeting Minna as the car loaded with her friends from Beverly Hills stopped to pick her up. "What are the pails for? You look like a milkmaid."

"And what did you expect to put the grunions in—your hat?" Minna ground her teeth. She would positively not get angry tonight and spoil her own fun, but she could not resist a gibe. At this hour of the night, Lucia was wearing a large straw hat swathed under her chin with a veil that matched her orange Capri pants. Terribly chic!

"You're the mariner. Now where do we go?" Harold was the driver, and he seemed the best of the lot of them. All the boys and girls were giggling and carrying on in a fashion that made Minna feel like a stranger—though they were all about her age—and certainly like a beachcomber. All but Harold were dressed to the teeth—the boys in Hawaiian shirts, the girls in something equally flimsy. Harold was wearing a sweater and clam-diggers that looked as though they had actually been used for digging clams.

As they unloaded at a stretch of beach where grunions might be expected, two were carrying portable radios playing full blast and several had flash lanterns with illumination as blinding as the headlights of a train. They were equipped, but not for grunions. Surest way to scare them off was to make a lot of noise and show lights. Grunions were elusive.

"I don't go so much for this grunion bit." One of the girls was already shivering. "Not without a moon. It's so awfully dark. Couldn't we have a fire?"

"We could, if we had come earlier." Minna was beginning to feel more and more like a girl scout leader. "We could have rubbed two boy scouts together." It was an old joke, and she had not expected anyone to laugh.

She helped Harold to spread out the blankets where everyone could sit and watch the blackness of the ocean. One could never tell about grunions. If one were lucky, they would spill from one of the larger waves in a silvery cascade. In the fraction of time before another wave carried them once more out into the ocean, the females would dig their tails in the sand and lay eggs which the males would fertilize.

Minna ended her explanation and waited an uncertain moment for the flippant comments she was sure would come from this sophisticated crowd. But she didn't hear them.

The picnickers were cuddling together for warmth

and watching the ocean. Cruising up and down the beach because she was bored with them, Minna kept close to the water. She was aware of dark forms on the sand that could be couples from other parties and none of her business.

"Sort of lonely for you, isn't it?" Harold joined her in her pacing.

"You mean what?"

"Well, you don't belong with this crowd, and you've only come to be nice."

"You could put it that way."

"And I think you're nice, too. And cute."

Harold had to spoil his compliment by putting his hand under her chin and kissing her straight on the mouth. "You like that, honey?"

"No, I don't." Minna wriggled free and slapped him. "You don't kiss a girl unless you mean it—and she does." She sat down on the sand and sobbed, "I hate you."

"Didn't mean a thing by it." Harold drew her to her feet.

"Th-that was just the trouble."

"I've kissed all sorts of girls." Harold was clearly puzzled by her reaction. "They usually like it."

"Well, I don't. I don't like it one single bit the way you did it."

It was then that the grunions, in their curious and unfathomable way, decided to descend. The first large wave had brought a few of them, but now a multitude were slithering across the sand.

"Bring a pail, someone." Minna was scooping grunions up by handfuls and tossing them behind her. "Don't just stand there."

The grunions were running, and so was the crowd. They were scrambling after the grunions, and the grunions were wriggling to escape. Pursuing them, Lucia lost her hat which, presumably, floated out to sea. No one was eager to swim after it to recover the silly old thing.

10

A Date With George

When Lucia's crowd departed for home a day or two later, Minna was relieved. She didn't want Harold hanging around and trying to play any more parlor games. Perhaps she was old-fashioned to feel that when a boy kissed a girl it ought to be special, but she had no wish to change. Lucia had prettier clothes than she had, and loads of dates, but as Minna went back to the familiar surroundings of Cliffside High she wouldn't have traded places with her cousin for anything in this world.

Some schools had spring vacation one week and some another, so that Easter bunnies still were lingering. Everybody at school had stories to tell about them. It was a chance for the Cliffside students to feel superior, and they made the most of it. Even Hans Van Der Oster made fun of the bunnies, and Bob Jones declared they ought to be exterminated.

Minna's one regret was that George Hartford's vacation hadn't coincided with hers, and that he was home when she had to trudge off to school. Her chances of encountering him were slight, except in the late afternoons. When she heard his front door slam, she was apt to make a dash up to the mailbox which stood on a post near the road, or she would go out in the front yard and pull crab grass.

"Got a crush, eh, sis?" Her brother Hugh was a junior at UCLA where George was a freshman, and he observed her antics with amusement. "How time flies. I thought you were still playing with dolls."

"That was last year," Minna said crossly, "and if you don't quit teasing me, I'll turn the hose on you."

Hugh had driven his old jalopy into the driveway to get it off the road before the trash-men dumped it by mistake, their father said. And now he was cleaning out the inside and washing it because he had a date.

George's car, parked across the road, was in little better shape, but to Minna it was an enchanted chariot and the youth who appeared to drive it a heavenly being in a T-shirt. Today, the car wouldn't start, and presently George was in a temper. He was an excitable sort; and now, as the engine growled feebly and finally died away altogether, he leaped out of the car and kicked it.

"Come on, you—help me give it a push," he shouted to Hugh, and to Minna who was watching his every movement. He was angular and lean with a face like an exclamation point, an impression increased today by the dark wiry hair that was standing on end.

"Needs more than a push, boy!" After a block, Hugh was panting with exertion and annoyance. He had his own car on which to work.

George raised the hood and began the tinkering that, as the minutes passed, called for half the tools from the garage. Minna fetched them, happy to be of use and to have this time with George. It was bliss to be a slave to George and to know that he needed her, if only to bring him the monkey wrenches.

"Wish I got that kind of service," Hugh remarked when she passed him on her way into the house to freshen her lipstick and spray her hair with cologne.

"You be still," Minna said absently, trying to decide whether to take the time to change into her more becoming pink sweater. Whatever could she do to make George notice her as a girl and not as "that little kid from across the street"?

All he said when she returned was that she had taken an age, and wasn't it just like a woman to disappear when you were counting on her. He wanted her to get into the front seat and try the starter while he held the connection to the battery, or something like that. The motor of a car was as much a mystery to Minna as how to attract George's attention.

He treated her like a sister, and one brother was enough for any girl.

What was there about one boy that could make you grateful just to be allowed to stay around him while he

for her, bouncing tennis balls against the door of his garage and being furious when he missed. George was often out-of-sorts and, for Minna, that was part of his charm. She did not care for boys who were stodgy and dull, she decided, including Bob Jones in this category. One always knew what Bob would do next, but George was unpredictable. She looked out of the window, lost in her daydreams, and floating upon the fluffy clouds of spring. " 'And when my heart with rapture fills, and dances with the daffodils.' "

This *would* be the afternoon when her Latin teacher asked her to stop by after class. He said that he wanted to talk to her about her grade. She was forced to wait while other students filed before him for private consultation. Some left in tears, and others with smiles. One never knew how one was going to fare in Latin because the teacher was pernickety and stiff. Parents said the school was lucky to have such a fine old scholar in it, but among themselves the students claimed he must have been there since the time of ancient Rome. He was a lover of the classics, and Minna was sure he never read a newspaper or went to a movie.

Now, as he looked at her sternly over his glasses, she knew that she was in for it. Her translations had been sloppy, her attention wandering.

"You've been slipping lately, Miss Vail," he said, addressing her formally, "and I'm sorry to see it. You showed promise last semester and the beginning of this one. It would be a shame for a possible A student to come

ment. Families had to live through it, and he had been no bargain himself when he was fifteen, as she recalled.

"Well, I don't know how you stand this kid around all the time. Glad I don't see much of her. She makes me sick." Hugh threw down his napkin and strode from the table.

Hugh might act like Mr. High-and-Mighty, but there were some things he didn't know. He thought that the girl he was taking out tonight was practically engaged to him, whereas Minna had seen her out with three different fellows. Also, she did not care to inform him that George had asked her to play tennis tomorrow after school.

She wouldn't tell Ciss and Betsy until afterward, when she might happen to drop a remark. It would be a long time before Laura would be back to share her innermost thoughts, but the doctors were giving more hope every day, Mr. Adams reported.

Tonight, for the first time, she might dare to write Laura a funny little note—nothing serious—but she found this hard to do. Anxiety still kept creeping into her words. She would, instead, find one of those amusing cards that covered racks in some of the stores and let it carry her message. The main thing, as Mother said, was to let Laura know that she was thinking about her. Usually, it took hours to pick out such a card because one had to read them all. She would have to wait until the day after tomorrow, because tomorrow was a special day.

All through her classes she pictured George waiting

worked on his old car that vibrated, now, like a milk shake? George's face was streaked with grease and perspiration—his dark eyes were flashing with impatience, as he ordered her to do this and do that, and made her like it. If it had been Bob Jones, she would have told him to go ahead and fix his old piece of junk by himself, but George was older—and George was different. He was almost nineteen, and last year he had been the idol of the high school.

Mother said he was spoiled by his mother and everyone else when Minna, in answer to her question, told how she had spent the latter part of the afternoon. This was nothing new—Minna had always liked George and enjoyed running errands for him.

"He has too much personality for his own good—or so he thinks," Hugh said with a meaningful glance at his sister. "Remember that."

"You're jealous because he has a better chance of getting to be the Octopus than you do!" Minna was hotly defensive. "Who'd ever vote for you—you old bookworm?"

"Now, now, children." Mother passed the biscuits with the mild remark that it was nice to help your neighbors, but one needn't overdo it.

"Not unless you're in love." Hugh was being horrid as only a brother could be, and Minna longed to slap him.

All girls Minna's age were in love with someone, Mother told Hugh. It was a natural stage of their develop-

out with a C or possibly a flunking grade. Now, wouldn't it?"

"Yes, sir, I'll try to do better." Minna flushed painfully. "I didn't know it was quite as bad as all that."

"It should be easy for you if you concentrate," the old man was never unkind. "Can't you try that, my dear?"

Minna promised that she would, and she meant it. She had been concentrating this spring but not in the direction of the classics. Last year and even this fall it had been easier to study. She could not explain to the gentle old scholar that when a girl started thinking so much about boys, nothing else seemed important. He had never been young, not ever, and he would not understand.

"Thank you, sir, for warning me. I'll try to do something about it before it is too late."

The school bus took her close to home, but it had left much earlier. She would have to wait for one of those city buses now, but they ambled along and never kept their schedules. Better to walk than to stand on a street corner expecting it. She could run between blocks and work off some of her impatience, even if she got so tired she could never beat George at tennis. She would run up panting to where George was waiting for her and, if not falling prettily into his arms, show a charmingly feminine confusion, as she pictured it. This might prove to be exactly the way to make George notice her as a girl, get him to fuss over her.

The setup seemed a perfect one except that neither

George nor his car were in sight. If he had been bouncing balls in expectation of her arrival, he had scooped them up and disappeared. Probably because she was late.

Drenched with perspiration and disappointment, Minna walked slowly down the steps that led to her own front door. She had failed George, and he had gone without her. He would never ask her to play tennis again. Weary of watching for his car to return so that she could explain, she lay down on her bed and was drifting into a nap when she heard voices, gay laughing voices, in front of the Hartfords' house.

She stepped outside and saw a line of cars, of assorted shapes and ages, about to disgorge a college crowd. George was directing traffic, showing them where to park along the narrow street, when he saw her.

"Hi, Minnow," he called to her. "Sorry about tennis today. I just thought of it. How about tomorrow?"

"I'll see if I can make it." Minna tried to keep her response cool and indifferent, but apparently George couldn't hear her.

"How's that again?" he shouted.

"Sure," she shouted back.

George had let her down but perhaps he hadn't meant to, she thought, trying to find excuses for him. He was absent-minded, but she wasn't today as she passed from class to class and raised her hand to answer questions. The Latin teacher had put her on the alert, and she realized that his criticism applied to most of her schoolwork. Her life was complicated enough without bringing home a poor report card and having to face the parental wrath that was sure to descend.

It had been so much simpler when all she had to think about was whether she had her themes in on time and got A's or B's, who said what to whom, and whether she should wear her red sweater or her green one. Though this was part of her recent past, it seemed as far away as her childhood. A dull, safe time as compared with the excitement of wondering now what boys, and George in particular, thought about her, or could be made to think.

When she saw him lounging about the door of the high school, she all but dropped her books with surprise. Two senior girls had taken possession of him, one on either arm; she tried to retreat before he could catch a glimpse of her. Her eyes blinded suddenly with tears, and she wanted to run away and hide. George had forgotten his date with her again, she was sure. He could not possibly have come up here to pick her up, not her, an insignificant sophomore who could not compete with these girls who were obviously adoring him.

The throng behind Minna, pressing to get out of school, pressed her on ruthlessly and made her face him without the benefit of so much as a handkerchief.

"What's the matter, Minnow? Have a bad day in class?" Unbelievably, George disentangled himself from the girls and put an arm around her. "Hurt somewhere?"

"N-Not where it shows." Minna struggled to regain her composure. She hated to be publicly conspicuous, have everyone notice her.

"Let's go get a hamburger, and you can tell me all about it." Mercifully George hurried her away. He was so kind and so tender that her tears welled afresh. How could she pour her troubles to the person who today was the cause of them?

"I d-don't want a hamburger," she wailed. "Take me home!"

"Best thing to do, I guess," he answered, patting her. "You wouldn't feel like playing tennis anyway."

He had gotten up to high school early, so he could take a look around, he said, adding that he rather missed the old place. He hadn't known what door she would use; but it was lucky that he had struck the right one, wasn't it?

Minna sat up, her cheeks still wet with tears, but her recovery miraculous. So George had planned to meet her after all! "I've changed my mind, and I do want a hamburger. That's just what I need to fix me up," she prattled, reaching into her purse for her compact and her lipstick. The girl who looked back at her from the small mirror had eyes that shone.

11

A Hot Chestnut

Once the echoes of the Easter bunny invasion had died away, Cliffside began to prepare for the great event of its year—the Carnival of the Sea. Everyone from the smallest kindergarten child up to spry octogenarians participated in it each summer, and plans must be laid well ahead. Each year the Chamber of Commerce offered prizes for the best jingles, best posters, best ideas for costumes and stunts. For a week in mid-July, ordinarily staid citizens would cavort to attract the tourists that were the lifeblood of Cliffside. The Carnival was a focus for publicity for the town in other parts of the country, and civic bosoms swelled because some inspired writer had compared it with the famous Mardi Gras in New Orleans.

"They must have paid him extra for that," Mr. Vail said when he heard about it. "I'm not going to make a fool of myself again this year, I can tell you that," he announced at the family dinner table.

"I thought you were awfully good with that red beard and all," Minna said loyally. "Red Beard, the pirate, getting everyone who wasn't dressed up to walk the plank in front of your hardware store."

"Didn't sell any more pots and pans and cans of paint than if I didn't."

Minna and her mother looked at each other, aware that he would never miss out on Carnival fun if he could help it.

"They're still counting on you for the Grunion troupe, I suppose." Mother knew that the question was still a sore point with Minna.

"They certainly are. I'm supposed to train all the little beasts to do handsprings, and start as of now. Did you ever hear of anything so silly?"

"Well, you can't do it all at the last minute." Mother did not add "—as you usually do everything," but Minna could tell by the tone of her voice that was what she meant. Sometimes you heard more when a person didn't say something than when they did.

"With sixty minutes to the hour and twenty-four hours to the day, and more than sixty days before the Carnival, I've got about a million minutes until then. So what's the rush?"

"Ninety thousand minutes in round numbers," her father corrected her.

Minna preferred not to think about the Grunion troupe in her waking moments, but sometimes in her dreams the imps came around to haunt her. There were dozens of them with devilish little faces and silver tails, all carrying spears and pricking her and chanting, "Minnow wants to be something she ain't—and she cain't, yah, yah."

Ciss and Betsy were never bothered deeply about the Carnival. They would be Sea Anemones again as they had last year—and the year before that. Dressed in skirts made of organdy petals, they would ride on Betsy's father's float, which advertised his lumberyard. "It's more fun that way," they always said. "You don't have to do anything."

They were talking about the Carnival at lunchtime, as who wasn't? The English classes were supposed to write jingles, and the art classes were to start drawing posters. The school band was practicing its numbers for the parade, and the glee club was already rehearsing to sing en masse things like "My Bonnie Lies Over the Ocean," and "Barnacle Bill," and "Rocked in the Cradle of the Deep."

A person would have to be dead and buried not to know that Cliffside was going to have a Carnival, but this year Minna was not enthusiastic. Without Laura to try out with her, she did not see how she would have the courage to face the judges when the time for choosing the Mermaids came. She would not dream of asking Betsy and Ciss; they would only laugh at her. They weren't mean, but they would think it was a joke. First thing one knew, the whole school would hear of it. "That Minnow Vail. Who does she think she is, anyway?"

A girl had to be pretty and preferably popular with the boys to stand a chance, and even then she might not win. Competition was stiff and, of the dozens of girls who had the nerve to appear before the judges in the big auditorium before a large audience, only ten could be selected for the coveted title. A girl had to have personality and be a "standout." Usually they were juniors and seniors and college girls. The age limit was twenty, and a girl couldn't be married, a model, or a professional beauty of any kind. Apart from these restrictions, any regular or summer resident of Cliffside could compete and parade across the stage while the audience and the judges picked their favorites. Like the Carnival, the Mermaid contest was a strictly amateur affair, given to choose the most attractive girls to serve as Neptune's court.

The nearest Minna would ever get to being a Mermaid was to swim like one she thought, as she went down to the beach for a dip. Now that the days were getting longer and the water warmer she could swim after school, and today Bob was joining her. Without any lifeguards yet on the beach at this season of the year it wasn't a good idea to go swimming by herself, and didn't she know that? Ever since the episode of the moray eel Bob had been protective.

The old Minna would have pooh-poohed this with an "I can take care of myself," but there were times now when a new Minna took over and thought twice before she spoke.

Today they discussed swimming out to the big rock

offshore where a male seal ruled like a sultan over his harem and fought off all other seals who tried to invade his realm. Some day he would be toppled from his throne by a younger, more powerful seal . . . . his kingdom was always an interesting state of commotion.

"We don't have our flippers or the rubber raft. Think you can make it?" Bob was dubious.

"I can if you can." Minna was stronger than she looked, but she was also apt to be daring and rash. Bob knew a good deal about Minna, but as his glance traveled over her slim, wiry little figure he apparently liked what he saw.

"You're a funny girl, do you know that, Minna?"

"And you're a funny boy."

Several big waves had crashed along the shore, and they should be followed by a period of calmer water. Minna was anxious to get out to sea, and she did not want to wait. Plunging in and swimming away from the shore, she was confronted by a mountain. The wave peaking above her was a monster and in the split moment before it broke she had to decide whether to try to dive beneath or cast her luck forward and hope to ride in with the crest. Either way was a gamble against the power of the sea.

Minna dived, and fortunately she made it out beyond, where the waves were only swells. "Isn't it exciting?" she called to Bob when he joined her.

"You do that once too often, Minna, and nobody's going to be around to pick you up." Bob was treading water, and his face was angry.

Minna's answer was a long easy side stroke out towards the rock. No need to hurry and use the crawl. If she got tired, she could float, turning herself into a little boat borne by the waves or propelled by her feet. She would like to stay in the ocean forever and never come back to shore, unless it were an exotic one where girls were dancing the hula. Would it be possible to float to the Hawaiian Islands and never return to Cliffside? She could go on forever and forever in this vastness of the blue and sparkling sea.

She was brave until a seal thrust its inquiring head above the water and circled them. A seal was a friendly creature with a bewhiskered face that was very like a dog's, but it was a reminder to Minna and Bob that they were farther out than they had ever gone before without the protection of their black rubber suits for warmth as well as for eluding possible sharks. Suppose it had been a shark's fin that had broken the water instead of the seal! Sharks were rare in this vicinity, but they were presumed to be interested in things in the water that were light in color such as bare arms and legs.

Sometimes one had a horrendous feeling when one realized that the ocean was fathoms deep below, and Minna had it now. She had been facing the open sea and its challenges, but now as she looked back and saw the cliffs far behind her, she felt herself to be a very small and helpless being.

"We'd better turn back, don't you think, Bob?" she

said, shivering. The seal rock was farther away than she had remembered, or than it had seemed from the shore today. Distances were deceiving in the ocean.

"Okay," Bob responded with alacrity, going into his crawl.

They raced each other most of the way to the beach and body-sledded in with the surf. It was good to feel the sand under her feet, Minna thought, good to rub down with a towel and jig up and down with Bob in their effort to get warm. It was better to do this with a boy—it increased your circulation. Boys were terribly important.

"I'm glad to see you're paying a bit more attention to Bob Jones these days," Mother said as a result of encountering them when Bob walked her home. "He's—well—possible."

"Could be," Minna affected the airy indifference she was practicing these days. She went into her room and saw that her wet hair made a cap about her face that, with dark red lipstick, was becoming. Even Minna decided it was, and she was her most critical audience. Bob Jones was possible. George Hartford was unattainable. And what girl wanted to settle for the possible?

"La-de-dah-dah," she hummed a tune as she came out to set the table for dinner. "What are we having for dinner? I'm dying."

Minna ate hungrily and asked for seconds and thirds, piling her biscuits high with butter and jam.

"I like to see a girl eat and not pick at her food, like your cousin Lucia." For Father, as for Minna, Lucia was a symbol of all that was wrong with the younger generation.

But Mother did not agree. It was too easy to blame Lucia when her parents were at fault. They had given her everything she wanted all of her life; never tried to control her. And now—Mother broke the news—they wanted the Vails to have Lucia for the summer. She was running wild, and the simpler life of Cliffside would be good for her, they thought.

"It isn't summer yet, by a long shot," Minna's father stabbed his fork into one of Mother's most expensive mats. "And why do they write to you when it's my business? Her father is my brother, remember."

"I'm quite aware of that, and a very different person, too." Mother reached for Father's hand, "Thank goodness."

"So now we're supposed to pick the hot chestnuts of *The Big Success* out of the fire? I won't have it, I tell you. My brother has made his own mistakes, and he can live with them." Father was what one might call livid.

Mother soothed him with a "No need to worry about it now." Lucia's parents were always changing their minds and could easily decide to send her off again to some expensive summer camp in the Rockies. Coming to Cliffside was only an idea they had suggested, but it need not be encouraged. They had had such ideas before, but they had come to nothing.

Minna's father ran his own hardware store in Cliffside, and his brother controlled a whole chain of supermarkets.

The difference between their incomes and their way of life was vast. Minna liked best a father who could put a sign on his store any time he liked—who could close it for the afternoon with GONE FISHING. That was the way merchants did things in Cliffside except during the summer season with its tourists.

Cliffside was different, and the Cliffside Vails were different, too. What the Beverly Hills Vails did was none of her father's problem, as he was careful to point out in some detail to her mother and to Minna. He didn't fly all over the country using credit cards, did he? He didn't dine on caviar and champagne. That was scarcely a meal, but Father used the extravagance of hyperbole when he was aroused.

Mother soothed him by suggesting a game of chess beside the fire. He could always beat her at chess. Minna, sensing a controversy that had gone on for a long while, but which she was faintly beginning to understand, whipped cream for the top of hot cocoa and sprinkled it with cinnamon. She would keep the fire piled high with the wood she had brought from the beach and not begrudge a stick of it. Nor would she insist upon her favorite television program which was coming on tonight and which would disturb the whole living room.

There were times when a daughter should disappear into her own room because she was tired. "All that swimming, you know." A daughter could be discreet and retire to put up her hair or wash it.

Peter accompanied her, mewing about her feet. He

wanted someone to play with him, old as he was. He was kittenish tonight, and frolicsome. If a person had Peter to chase and then to cuddle, one did not need any of those silly stuffed animals that Lucia always kept about her room.

12

Hospital Call

As the weeks passed and Laura still remained in the hospital up in Los Angeles, Minna felt more and more lost without her confidante. The Adamses were very encouraged about her and said she was "responding well to therapy." But they did not wish to push their luck too far, they said, and bring her home while the hospital "with all its facilities and modern methods" could speed her recovery.

"It won't be complete, I'm afraid," Mrs. Adams told Mother. "There may be a lasting paralysis, but," her face brightened, "the fact that we still have her is a miracle. And perhaps there will be others."

Laura could have visitors now and would love to see Minna. She was always talking about her and wondering what was going on at Cliffside High; perhaps Minna could drive up to Los Angeles with the Adamses one of these days. It was an idea, but Minna had another.

Bob had always liked Laura, and he had recently acquired his driver's license. Laura would enjoy seeing him, and it would be more of an occasion to make the journey with him than with Laura's parents. If Minna bought the gas, would he furnish the rest of the transportation?

When Bob scowled, Minna did not know that he had seldom driven on the freeway to the city and was unsure of himself. "If it's too much bother, I'll ask someone else." Minna was trying to practice new techniques on boys, and she had hoped Bob would be flattered by her request. Somewhere she had read that it was smart to give a boy a chance to show off.

"It isn't that I don't want to, Minnow, it's . . ." Bob hesitated. "Oh, all right, I will. If Dad will let me take the car, that is."

With Mother's permission, Minna stripped the garden of its roses and pondered what else to take to Laura. Magazines? Cookies? Books? "It's your visit that will count with Laura," Mother said, "knowing that you care enough to come. What you bring doesn't matter."

Minna packed a lunch so that she and Bob could eat it on the way. When you were asking a favor of a boy, she thought, you didn't expect him to spend money on you, too. She had risen early Saturday to make all her preparations, and by ten she was beginning to watch the clock and listen for the sound of his horn. Whatever was delaying him? She inspected her nail polish again and was adjusting the ribbon on her ponytail for the dozenth time when he appeared, wearing the suit he must have kept for Sundays.

Minna couldn't recall ever having seen him in a suit with a white shirt and a necktie. He looked years older and almost handsome, with a pleasantly masculine smell about him of barbershop cologne. His hair was freshly cut, and he had a white handkerchief neatly folded in his pocket. Altogether he had the appearance of a young man about town, and Minna's face showed her surprise.

"Can't always be a Cliffside hick, you know." He reached for the flowers and the lunch and escorted her into the car, opening the door for her with a gesture that was rare for a high school boy. With his attire, he had also donned his manners.

"You look pretty nice yourself," he said as Minna adjusted the halo of daisies and straw that was her only hat. Dress was so casual in Southern California that she seldom needed either a hat or gloves, but this was a trip up into the big city and, like Bob, she felt the need of acquiring that metropolitan look. Her navy blue flannel blazer was new, and so was her blue and white checked skirt; it had been her Easter outfit, and she wanted to show it to Laura, along with the black patent leather pumps that had three-inch heels.

"I declare, I hardly know us, do you?" she laughed to Bob as he handed her the road map. "And what am I supposed to do with this? Don't you know where we're going? Los Angeles, not San Francisco."

"Oh, sure, sure." Bob headed out one of the canyons that led in the direction of the freeway. Minna was glad she had thought of this expedition on their own which, surprisingly, both sets of parents had approved. Probably because it was "in a worthy cause." Minna was sick and tired of being a child who always had to be driven by her family, and today even the hills looked different to her. Usually so scorched and yellow, they were green with the flush of spring rains, and the new leaves of sycamores and willows along the trickles of the creeks were twinkling in the sunlight. Except where there were irrigation ditches or watered gardens, the vegetation in this part of Southern California was sparse, even in the spring; but Minna knew nothing of the lush landscapes of the East. This was home, and she loved it.

Once they were on the freeway, she realized that Bob was as nervous as she was about the maelstrom of traffic into which they had plunged. Cars were darting here and there, changing lanes, and honking at anyone who was a slow or uncertain driver.

"Don't mind them, Bob," Minna tried to reassure him. "Do what you think is best. They don't own the freeway."

"Yeh, but they think they do." Bob swerved to avoid a car that had cut in just ahead of his bumper.

"We should have stayed in Cliffside." Minna had never liked the freeway even when her father was driving.

"Fine time to think of that." Bob hung grimly to the wheel while Minna looked out at the dreary districts through which they were passing as they came nearer to Los Angeles; rows upon rows of houses of dingy pink or yellow stucco with scarcely a tree to break the monotony or lend beauty anywhere. How dreadful it would be to live here, and yet hundreds of people did. She and Bob were lucky to have Cliffside, she thought, switching on the car radio.

The radio would help to pass the miles which seemed endless. She had forgotten how long it took to drive up to Los Angeles with nothing worth looking at except an occasional view of the mountains where they lifted above the smog. Here and there a line of palm trees standing like disconsolate storks, now a dry and neglected orange grove awaiting the oncoming of the real estate developers who would advertise their tracts as "Aladdin's Castles" or some such nonsense.

"You said we had to turn off at Soto, didn't you?" Bob broke one of their many silences.

Minna looked through her purse for the scribbled list of directions which the Adamses had given her. Vermont was the turnoff, but where was it? You had to figure it out well ahead, or you would get stuck in the middle lane and go clear through to Hollywood. "Well, look at the map, can't you?" Bob gritted his teeth. The freeway was enough to put anyone in a temper.

When finally they arrived at the hospital after a dozen misdirections on Minna's part through the twists and turns and one-way streets of the city, they were not on speaking terms. According to Bob, Minna could not find her way through a wet paper bag. They had the number of Laura's room, but Bob would not even stop at the hospital desk to ask how to find it.

"Follow me," he strode on ahead to take the nearest elevator no matter where it led. Minna didn't say a word when they were almost immediately lost, cruising down one wing of the hospital and then another and, as she told Ciss and Betsy later, practically into the delivery room.

The hospital was a vast and confusing city in itself with strange sounds, weird echoes, moans, and cries. "So long as you look as though you know where you're going, they won't stop you," Bob flung over his shoulder as he opened a door and stepped into a laboratory filled with howling dogs and monkeys in cages and scurrying white rats and mice. "Hello, Laura." Minna went over to greet one of the chimpanzees.

She dreaded to see her friend in one of the hundreds of rooms which they had passed, perhaps with her leg suspended in mid-air, and screens about her bed. Except when she had had her tonsils out, Minna herself had never been in a hospital and this tremendous cavern of the sick appalled her.

"Oh, yes, Laura Adams." Finally they seemed to have reached the right floor and the right corridor. A nurse at the desk gestured toward a porch at the farther end. "I think you'll find her out there."

"You go first and tell me, Bob," Minna hung back. She had come all this way with her roses, but if her friend looked awful she would not be able to force so much as a smile. Probably, she would burst into tears. Far from being a help, she would be a mess.

"Hi, there, buddy." Minna heard a faint but familiar voice and saw a figure in a wheel chair coming toward her, with Bob behind and pushing it. Laura was still Laura, though she was thin and white and had her legs covered with a shawl. "If I wanted to reduce, I picked a fine way of doing it, didn't I?"

"Sure did, you look gorgeous." Hugging Laura couldn't do her any harm, could it? All the nurse had warned them against was staying too long and overtiring the patient.

"I'm swimming every day in the pool they have here, and soon I'm going to be able to beat you, Minnow."

"Do tell," Minna tried to keep her voice steady. It was a time for babbling, and so she did . . . about who dated whom in high school, and how ghastly Latin was and how her cat had learned a new trick and how they were making such a fuss over the Carnival this year you wouldn't believe it. Things like that. Betsy and Ciss both had different hairdos, and everyone was going mad over a new shade of nail polish and lipstick, being sure that they matched.

Bob listened with a boy's amused tolerance but put in a word now and then. He found several vases for the roses and helped Laura from her wheel chair into her bed. The nurse had flashed a warning glance that their time was almost up.

"You're going to try out to be a Mermaid, aren't you?" Laura's hand, reaching for Minna's, was all bones but all spirit. "You've got to, you know, for both of us."

"Sure thing," Bob's voice was hearty, "and I'll help. Don't worry about a thing, Laura."

Laura wouldn't, and she would be home again very soon. The doctors were promising her this.

"We'll be up every night to beat on the bongo drums," Bob said, referring to the jungle sounds made by the Easter bunnies. "We'll all get thrown out of Cliffside."

" 'By now." Laura and Minna said it together, quite as though Laura were sprawling on her own bed with the scarlet telephone and Minna were incarcerated in the hall closet.

" 'By, now."

Bob had taken the nearest door marked EXIT, and now they were facing a fire escape, a sort of chute that presumably led to the ground. Bob was game to try it if Minna was, and presently they found themselves in a parking lot that had no sign whatever of his father's car. They would seem to have lost it among all those signs that said DOCTORS ONLY and AMBULANCE and GARBAGE TRUCKS.

Somehow it was all Minna's fault, and it was up to her to find the car. When finally they did, they were both laughing. The hospital had been grim, and they had to laugh.

"What about going on to Olvera Street?" Bob asked. "If you've got the money, I've got the taste for *tortillas*."

Olvera Street was a quaint bit of very old California preserved in the heart of Los Angeles. The old adobes held curio shops and shops where they had cauldrons of wax with candles being dipped by hand. There were cobblers sewing on shoes, there were tinsmiths, and there were kitchens redolent with the smell of good Mexican food, of *tortillas* and enchiladas, of meat and of cheese. In the stalls that ran down the middle of the street, you could buy anything from a tiny Chihuahua dog to a hat with a miniature Mexican village on it. Strolling players draped in serapes strummed on their guitars . . . phonographs wailed with the sounds of *La Paloma.* Olvera Street was gay, and it was colorful and fun to visit. Especially with Bob.

Minna had never been there except with her parents who did not enter into the spirit of Olvera Street. Usually they were showing guests around, guests who wondered whether it was all hygienic and whether it wouldn't be wiser to settle for club sandwiches up at the Statler Hotel.

Bob had bought a gardenia from one of the flower stands, and it was fragrant in her hair. "You have a pretty girl, yes?" the man had said.

13

Minna—Model!

Minna seemed forever to be washing her sweaters and shaping them on towels to dry. She was always rinsing out blouses and lingerie and wondering whether there was a run in her last pair of nylons. She never wore nylons to school, but she would definitely have to have them for tonight to wear with her newly acquired three-inch heels.

Bob had asked her to a party that one of his crowd was giving. Probably a bore, Minna thought, remembering the last boy-and-girl party she had suffered through years ago. They had all been ten or eleven, and they had played "Post Office."

Ciss was going, too, and Betsy was pretending that she didn't care that no one had invited her. The other two knew differently; it was no fun to be left out and sit home alone on a Friday night or baby sit for the neighbors. If Betsy were willing to go with Hans Van Der Oster, Minna was sure she could arrange it. He wouldn't have the nerve to ask a girl himself, and even if he were still hard to talk to, he was a marvelous dancer.

Urged by her friends, Betsy agreed. It wasn't as though any of the three were going to have what one might call a romantic date, and pair off, and sit in corners holding hands. This wasn't to be that kind of a party. "Just a mob asked in for hot dogs and Cokes," Bob had said.

The next thing for the three of them to decide was what to wear. Ciss had a new pair of orange Capris, and perhaps she could borrow her older sister's gold thongs. Betsy had a muu-muu that was slinkier and much dressier than most; her aunt had sent it to her from Hawaii, and it had a butterfly bow in back. Minna's heels, of which she was so proud, would look best with her full striped chintz skirt and her peasant blouse. Anyone could wear anything to a Cliffside party, Ciss's sister had told her, and probably most of the boys would be in sport shirts and cords.

Minna had never been to the boy's house where the party was being held. From the look of him around high school, one might expect him to live in a beach shack and not in the beautiful Japanese style dwelling built on a terrace that overlooked the ocean. The rooms were partitioned off with sliding screens, some filled with a lovely pattern of butterflies and grasses, and everywhere she saw low tables and bright cushions on which to sit. Music was playing in the house and on the patio where most of the crowd was gathering, and where Minna thought she would feel more at home. The inside of the house was too elegant to be messed up by a mob of high school kids eating hot dogs with mustard.

She hadn't known this was to be a sort of political rally, and apparently Bob hadn't either. Ralph Roberts, whose guests they were, was boosting himself to be the next Octopus. His father was an advertising man, and doubtless it was he who had put up the banner across the patio that read VOTE FOR ROBERTS AND BE RIGHT. There were other signs on sticks, and everyone was supposed to pick one up and join the parade across the patio and out into the street for a snake dance.

"This is some kind of a party," Minna said loud enough to be heard by the woman who was serving up hot dogs and buns and who was doubtless Ralph's mother. "I think you're wrong with Roberts."

"It's only for fun, my dear," the woman answered her smoothly. "Only an icebreaker to get you young people acquainted."

Minna was unconvinced, and so were Bob and the others who gathered in tight little groups. Ralph and his father could take their high-powered promotion somewhere else; it wouldn't work in Cliffside.

You couldn't buy votes—not even with an elaborate cake made in the shape of an octopus. Each of the eight legs was frosted in a different color, and the eyes in the center were lights that flashed off and on—red and green. They had a bin full of small octopuses with springy legs that made them look more like spiders and they were giving them out as favors.

"Why don't you run against him, Bob?" Minna added her voice to the general murmur of protest. "You can be a candidate just as well as he can and—and there's a table over there where you can make your first speech." She urged him toward a sturdy piece of redwood furniture that could serve as his platform. With some reluctance, Bob allowed himself to be pushed forward, and then he leaped lightly upon the table and raised his arms.

"Listen, you guys and gals—I want to tell you there's a lot of us around here and a lot of good fellows and—and—" Bob hesitated, embarrassed because everyone had stopped their private conversations to listen. "Why don't you vote for me and 'Jelly with Jones'?"

"Hear! Hear!" The crowd stomped and whistled and clapped. "Hear! Hear!"

Not to be outdone by Bob, one chap after another took over his place on the table top, and campaign speeches became hilarious. "I may be a shrimp, but I want to be an Octopus!" and "Come into my arms, girls, for a genu-wine Octopus squeeze." If the Robertses had intended to break the ice they had succeeded in full measure. Whatever one might think about Ralph and his elaborate attempt at electioneering, his party was far from the bore that Minna had dreaded. It was actually a lot of fun.

When the din had subsided, a few couples started

dancing to the music that had been playing softly all the while. They were couples who were known to be "going steady"; but when Hans took the floor with Betsy, most stopped to watch them. He was such an excellent dancer that other boys looked like sticks by comparison, and Betsy was floating as though she were in a dream world.

She was a graceful little thing, but with a good partner like Hans almost any girl could feel like thistledown. Other girls clamored around wanting to dance with him, while the majority of the other boys stood around awkwardly, eating hot dogs and not wishing to compete against him.

Minna had never danced with Bob and if he wouldn't ask her now, she and Ciss would try the cha-cha together. Other girls were dancing together, also, until Mrs. Roberts decided to break up the stag line by "passing the broom." According to rules, if a girl gave a boy the broom he had to dance with her. As the broom passed from hand to hand, all the boys were forced out of their corners, and everyone relaxed and had fun.

Fathers started coming for some of the girls at twelve, and Minna had orders to be home shortly after that. The party broke up early, but not without a lot of calling back and forth in the street and plans for other parties. Boys who wanted to beat Roberts for Octopus all intended to give their own parties. It sounded as though there would be a whole series of them between now and Election Day, if parents didn't have different ideas. Ralph had started the ball, or the band wagon, or whatever it was, rolling.

Mr. Vail chuckled when Minna told him about it and said that some six-year-old probably would get it into his head now to run for Octopus and bribe his playmates with ice-cream cones and lollipops. Customarily the Octopus was some boy in his late teens or early twenties, and according to Mr. Vail's recollection, sophomores always before had been content to sit on the side lines and watch the spectacle.

"This year is different," Minna said. And it was—for her.

She was helping Bob plan his own party and, forgetting her shyness about talking to boys she scarcely knew, was enthusiastically inviting juniors and even seniors to it. She was backward, though, about Bob's telling anyone of her wish to be one of the Mermaids. She had sworn him to secrecy that night as they drove home from the visit to Laura, explaining that she knew she didn't have a chance. "Anyway, not this far ahead, Bob," she had pleaded when Bob loyally said he knew a lot of fellows who would back her up, or he'd certainly know the reason why.

"You're a funny girl, Minna." Bob used this phrase whenever she puzzled him.

In the present excitement over his sudden candidacy for Octopus, he apparently had dropped the matter, but Minna wondered who was responsible for her phone call from one of the Cliffside artists. The woman's voice sounded pleasant on the phone, but Minna had never met her. She was working on several posters for the Carnival contest, she said, and wanted Minna to come up and pose for her some afternoon.

"You might be the type I am looking for," Mrs. Forbes said, not explaining how she had come upon either Minna's name or her phone number.

"Wh-why—" Minna was too taken by surprise to ask. And she was also flattered, as what girl wouldn't be? "Why, sure."

She was bursting with curiosity by the time she found the woman's studio off one of the twisting byways that was little more than a path between stone walls ablaze with bougainvillaea. It was a quaint little shingled cottage set far back in the trees. As Minna skipped across the flagstone patio, around a bird bath and huge glass bottles placed where they would catch the light, she could smell paint through the half-open Dutch door.

Instead of working on some masterpiece, however, the spare little woman inside was engaged in putting the finishing touches on a row of large papier-mâché sea horses for one of the Carnival floats. She gestured for Minna to sit down on a big old upholstered chair with the stuffing running out of it. "I'll be through in a minute, and then we can talk."

Minna felt that the woman was appraising her, and she was certain of this when she was asked to take the ribbon from her ponytail and let her hair fall down over her shoulders. She was not sure how one posed for an artist.

Awaiting instructions, she tucked her foot under her and watched Mrs. Forbes.

"Don't move—I want to catch you that way." Mrs. Forbes dropped her paintbrush and, picking up a pad and a bit of charcoal, started to sketch with quick, broad strokes. As she finished one sketch, she began another and another until Minna begged to look.

"Comments disturb me until I have finished." Mrs. Forbes had an artist's temperament, but she offered Minna cookies and allowed her to relax for a few moments before she resumed her pose.

The pile of sketches beside the artist's bench had grown into a tantalizing heap before Minna was finally permitted to leap up and examine them. And then she was delighted.

The drawings were loose and fanciful, but Minna was clearly recognizable as a mermaid seated not upon this beaten old chair but upon the edges of beautiful shells and, in some of the variations, within the mysterious depths of sea caves. The mermaid Mrs. Forbes had portrayed was not a voluptuous siren but a young and wistful girl whose eyes were filled with dreams.

"Yes, they're quite successful," the artist agreed. "Too good for posters, really. I may adapt a few of them to this medium, though, and enter the others in the art show. Now let's try something a little bit more obvious, shall we?"

She decided that one of the sea horses was dry enough to use as a prop. Minna was to sit on a high stool and dangle her legs over its back, like a mermaid riding side-saddle, while she held up an arm and maintained a frozen smile. Mrs. Forbes was a hard taskmaster, asking almost as much of her model as she did of herself. She was working with pastels and trying various color combinations when Minna, tremulous, asked whether this might be enough for one afternoon. She could come back tomorrow or. . . .

"This is the best of them, don't you think so?" The artist did not bother to answer Minna's question, but held up a stylized form of Minna with blond hair streaming against a dark blue sea. The sea horse was orange, and the effect was strong and dramatic.

As Minna came over to her side to review the collection, Mrs. Forbes admitted that she was too tired to make any sensible choice. "Thank you, my dear. That boy was right. I wanted to do something fresh and young with a different type of model. However could he have known that you would answer what I had in the back of my mind?"

"What boy?"

"Why, Bob Jones, of course. Who else?"

So this was the solution to the riddle. Mrs. Forbes was an old friend of Bob's mother, she explained, and she had promised Bob that she would get several posters done before his party. So he could show them there. "I can't imagine why, can you?"

"Yes, I can." Minna had not realized how clever Bob could be. Without telling her, he had gotten her drawn as a mermaid by this excellent artist. No one who came to his Octopus party could mistake that this was she—Minnow Vail—and that she made a most effective mermaid who might be worthy of their support.

14

Company Coming

With so many boys now wooing for the Octopus vote, it would have been difficult for any girl to be a wallflower in Cliffside that spring. If you were supporting one boy, you went to all the others' parties to join in the general merriment, and even oldsters were taking sides. Everyone in the town old enough to write his name would have a vote on election day. The list of candidates would probably narrow down before then, but now it was still a free-for-all.

Mr. Vail, who was on the Chamber of Commerce committee, complained that if people would give as much toward street decorations as they were spending on these affairs for their sons there would be no problem at all in turning the main thoroughfares into a "bower of glory." As for himself, Minna was asking for so many new outfits that he was, to hear him tell it, headed for the poorhouse.

When Father was emphatic, the old timeworn expressions were good enough for him.

"She doesn't spend much on any one of them," her mother defended her, "and she has to be in the swim."

"I liked it better when she was doing it in a bathing suit."

Minna left them discussing her as she went into her room to do her homework. With not very many weeks left of school, the teachers were loading them down with assignments, and everyone was complaining about it. It was a time, too, when she could raise her grades and not seem completely the family dunce as compared to Hugh. He had always gotten straight A's in high school and was nearly equaling this record at UCLA where he had won a scholarship that would send him for the summer to another university. The thought of Hugh put her on the same campus with George Hartford, and she sighed.

George hadn't been home for what seemed ages, and his mother said he was busy with track events. "You know, the high hurdles." George would never settle for the low ones, Minna agreed, picturing George streaking down the field ahead of everyone else. George was George, and there was no one else at all like him. She found the newspaper picture of him taken last year when he was president of the senior class and still kept hidden in the bottom drawer of her bureau.

Soon she would be able to discuss him again with Laura, for Laura at last was coming home. She was pining for her home and her friends, her parents said; the doctors felt that these would do more for her than a longer stay in the hospital, which was a lonely place. Minna agreed; she didn't see how Laura had been able to stand it as long as she had, so far from everything and everyone she loved. She would go up to see Laura every day, and sometimes twice, she decided in an excess of enthusiasm, forgetting the distance afoot. Betsy would go, and Ciss, and lots of others . . . everyone wanted to see Laura. For the next few days, the prospect of her return was the main topic of conversation at lunch.

"Too bad she can't get in on any of these parties we're having," Ciss remarked thoughtfully. "Maybe it would make her feel worse if we tell her about them. Maybe we shouldn't."

"What else is there to talk about these days?" Betsy cracked the shell of her hard-boiled egg on the table and slowly picked off the pieces as she considered the problem. "Examinations? Television? Cleaning out the garage?"

Minna said that Laura wasn't to be shielded. Mrs. Adams had told Mother that they were supposed to treat her like a normal girl. She wasn't to be fussed over and babied, the doctors advised. She had been taught to do a great many things for herself in the hospital, and most of what was wrong with her now was that she couldn't walk. Her arms were all right, but it was her legs that were paralyzed, maybe permanently and maybe not.

"I should think that was enough," Ciss said in her forthright fashion. "I feel awfully sorry for her."

Again Minna remembered what Mrs. Adams had mentioned to her mother. Laura was positively not to be pitied, and a person was not supposed to mention her handicap unless she did.

"It will be hard at first, I guess, but we'll get used to it." Betsy took out her purse and counted the pennies so as to be sure she had enough for milk from the machine. "If it will be good for Laura, we'll have to."

Maybe it would be better if they all went together the first time, the three girls agreed. Then there wouldn't be any of those awkward silences; some one of them could think of something to say to fill in the gaps. "She really doesn't look so bad," Minna tried to reassure them, but inwardly she dreaded this first encounter on home ground as much as the others did. In the hospital, a wheel chair seemed a quite natural vehicle with so many patients riding around in them, but it might be a different matter in the Adamses' living room.

Like Ciss and Betsy, she was all but rehearsing her opening lines by the time they got to the Adamses' front door and rang the bell. Billy, surprisingly clean and combed and courteous, answered it. "Come in and sit down," he said. In other days, he was apt to slam the door in their faces. Billy had changed.

When Laura appeared, she was wearing a muu-muu that fell down over her feet, and she was operating the wheel chair herself. "Like my kiddie car?" she asked, making a joke that put all of them more at their ease.

"Do you have a driver's license?" This was from Betsy. "Any trouble with flat tires?"

"Ever been arrested for speeding?"

The girls had taken their cue from Laura, and nothing serious was said. Presently they were chattering like magpies. It was almost like the old days except that Billy appeared presently with lemonade and cookies which, obviously, he had fixed by himself. The glasses were oddly assorted and the cookies were soggy where the lemonade had spilled on them.

"He's a nice kid," Laura said, and the others agreed with her heartily.

Mrs. Adams was nowhere in sight, and Laura said she had gone into town on an errand. Billy was in charge, and as he appeared several times in the doorway with an anxious expression they knew it was time to leave.

"For a kid of ten, he's doing all right," Ciss said, breaking the silence as they walked away down the hill.

Laura still had her red telephone, and she could talk on it any time. Her voice was getting stronger, Minna noticed. It had at first seemed faint and faraway. You could tell a lot about a person by the sound of the voice on the phone, Mother said when Minna remarked about it. Minna was not getting up to the Adamses' even once a day, as she had intended. She felt guilty about this, but she simply couldn't make it. There were so many other things she had to do during these last weeks of school, so much that was pressing on her.

She was having to train the Grunion troupe though she loathed it. She was having to be nice to all sorts of strange and assorted boys because they might vote for Bob. And, now that summer was coming on apace, Mother needed her as an extra clerk in the gift shop.

All this was hard to explain to Laura when she chatted with her on the phone every night. Laura must be bored silly, sitting up there on the hill and doing nothing but knit and go to her hydrotherapy. Minna wished that somehow she could make it better for Laura, but she could not think of a way.

"Don't try so hard, dear," Mother told her, referring not only to Laura but to everything in general. "The world doesn't rest on your shoulders."

To Minna, it did. She wanted to be everywhere all at once doing everything right. Every single thing. Nobody did, her mother reminded her, nobody did. She was like the man in the old story who got on his horse and wanted to ride off all at once in all directions.

Worst of all, Lucia was going to spend the summer in Cliffside—that was now definite—and Minna would have to share her room with her cousin. They had not done this for years, except for a day or so during Christmas holidays, and Minna loathed the whole idea. When they were small she and her cousin had been like sisters, but of recent years they had grown as far apart as the different lives they led.

Father had said repeatedly that Lucia could be "wished" on them only "over my dead body," but he was still in debt to his brother for a large part of the sum he had borrowed to buy the hardware store and go into business for himself. Except for a fortunate few, most people did not make much money in Cliffside; they were there for the pleasant life. It was a low-pressure sort of place and one that a high-pressure man like Minna's uncle was apt to call a "one-horse town."

Besides, as Mother reminded Father, families had obligations to each other that went far deeper than money. Lucia needed calming down, needed a chance to get away from her city associates and be in a "home atmosphere." Summer camps were impersonal and had not supplied the answer her parents were seeking.

"I'm not sure that we have it either, but I can't see that it will hurt any of us to try," Mother said. Had Father forgotten the time when she had been so ill and Minna had been tenderly cared for months on end up in Beverly Hills?

"Minna was a baby then, and it was an emergency." Father knew that he was fighting a battle already lost.

Lucia would be arriving very soon because the private school she attended let out early so that, according to Father, families could go out on their yachts or off to Europe. Both Minna and her father had a highly-colored idea of life among the rich.

Lucia probably would want three-fourths of the closet space for all her clothes, and most of the drawers. "I might as well move out into the garage," Minna said crossly to Mother who, in turn, suggested that Minna could make room for three girls if she threw out even half of her "junk." Mother called it "junk"—all the piles of old magazines, trunks of dolls and doll clothes, old letters and souvenirs and clothes that someone had given her and which she and Mother were going to "make over" on some day that never arrived. Minna was a collector, and her room resembled the nest of a magpie.

Mother was getting new corduroy covers in turquoise for each of the twin beds and making new curtains in a bright shade of red that Minna had selected. They would be cafe-style with brass rings to slide over the rods, and they would replace the old draperies Minna had inherited when Mother did over the living room. Her room had been shabby, but neither Mother nor Minna had given a great deal of thought to this until now. It was high time something was done about it, they both agreed. Regardless of Lucia's visit, it was high time.

"Anyone would think we were expecting Queen Elizabeth," Father said, bringing home reading lights from his store that could be attached to each of the beds.

Mother was dyeing the small loopy cotton rugs red to match the curtains. They had been a dingy white that was disgraceful, and she had long been meaning to change them. The painted walls could be washed, and Mother and Minna had found enchanting wallpaper to cover one end of the room. It depicted a street scene in Paris, and Mother thought of adding tiny artificial blooms here and there on the flower stands, gluing them for an effect that impressed even Father who had been ordered into service to hang the wallpaper. He decided then that the beat-up old furniture which Minna had acquired from various other changes in the house looked horrible and helped to paint it all with white enamel.

It was a matter of family pride to spruce up before Lucia's arrival, but Minna adored the result. Her room looked almost like something out of one of the magazines, instead of a catchall old dump.

Lucia was due almost any day now and, try as she might, Minna could not forget about that. Whatever would she do with her cousin when her own classes were still in session? And wherever could she go for privacy all summer long? Minna, raised alone, resented this intrusion more than she had mentioned to either her mother or her father. Like the beach, her room was her retreat from everything that bothered her. Now she would have only the beach. A girl needed to think sometimes, and she could do it only when she was by herself.

15

Lucia Takes Over

Sitting on a rock above the ocean, Minna postponed going home tonight as long as she could. Her uncle and aunt would have driven down from Beverly Hills to bring Lucia, and her mother had prepared to have a dinner far more elaborate than it usually was. But, as Minna knew from previous occasions, there would be a great deal of conversation and delay beforehand. She and Mother had set the table the previous night, and Minna had prepared the salad greens before she left for the beach. Now she would rush in at the last possible moment, too late for anyone to remark how she had grown. There must be a time when one outgrew even this, but Minna had not yet come to it. She would hear quite enough as it was of "how nice for the girls to spend the summer together" and "take care of our precious darling."

Precious darling could take care of herself, so far as

Minna was concerned, at least until her own school ended. She could just go to the library and read a book, couldn't she? Cliffside was not an amusement park run by one Minna Vail for the benefit of her cousin Lucia.

Minna was conducting a conversation with herself in which the sea gulls were not interested. Circling overhead or alighting upon the beach to search for remnants of left-over picnic lunches, the gulls had their own preoccupations—as did a flight of pelicans, low above the sea. Out on a farther rock, a cormorant stood in lonely silhouette against the sky, watching for fish. The sunset was fading, and it was almost night.

From long habit, Minna gathered up what pieces of firewood the ocean had brought. Even in summer, there were some chilly nights when one needed a fire. She was discriminating about her choice of the fuel; pieces must not be too long or Father would have to saw them in two, a chore he disliked. They must not be too thin, or they would burn out too fast. Lucia would know nothing whatever about what wood was suitable to carry, and doubtless she would not bother with it anyway. It was often sticky and covered with oil, as it was tonight.

Minna would look to be a proper beachcomber unless she stopped in the garage and found turpentine to remove the tarry substance splotched over her arms. But tonight, rebellious, Minna decided that she didn't care. She would present herself just as she was, black goo, old gray sweat shirt and all. Mother wouldn't scold in front of guests, and they could see for themselves what their darling daughter might become if she remained in Cliffside. It was an audacious last-stand attempt on Minna's part to get them to take Lucia away with them.

To her surprise, Lucia looked worse than she did. Her hair had not been combed in weeks, or so it appeared. Her mother said it was part of the French influence, or was it Italian? Gamin, way out, wild. And Lucia was wearing what in Cliffside would be called a gunny sack. It fit like one—a thing made of two colors of burlap and fringed at the bottom.

These girls of ours—parents regarded them both with an expression of fond amusement.

Minna had avoided taking Lucia to high school with her until one of the last days when she could think of no further excuses that would hold water with Mother. Mother knew that classes were all but finished, and students were more or less sitting around twiddling thumbs and waiting for the final word that would release them for the summer. Minna had complained about this last year, and Mother had remembered. There had been no Octopus parties since Lucia's arrival, and Minna had been able to keep her cousin more or less under wraps.

Now Mother was saying that none of the teachers could object to a guest in the classroom when they were largely occupied with checking on projects and making out grades. It would be a good chance for Lucia to meet Minna's friends. Exactly, Minna ground her teeth—exactly what she had been trying to avoid.

Lucia was wearing pink checked gingham with innumerable petticoats. There were so many of them that they bounced into the aisles beyond the various seats where Minna had placed her. It wasn't that girls in Cliffside didn't have petticoats, but that Lucia did not bother to control them. And her hair was *still* in disorder. She was bored in classes, she sulked prettily, and everyone noticed her.

Ciss and Betsy were polite to her at lunch because she was Minna's cousin, but conversation was chilly and forced. Lucia picked at the tuna fish sandwiches with the air of one who was used to lobster and, drawing a cosmetic bag from her purse, proceeded to try several different shades of eye shadow which she offered around the table, with eyebrow pencil and mascara and a curler for the lashes. She was making it all too clear that, since they were only girls together, there was nothing to talk about and nothing to do but beautify. "I don't suppose you smoke," she said, drawing a cigarette from her case and preparing to light it.

"You do that, and you'll get thrown out of school." Minna forgot that her cousin couldn't be, since she was not a Cliffside student. "It's against the rules."

"So many quaint little customs," Lucia gave a little laugh and replaced the cigarette with candy mints.

Lucia was a girl who was very unsure of herself. Mother had said this to Father, and Minna had overheard the remark. So Lucia was unsure of herself, and who wasn't? It did not give her an excuse to be insufferable.

"You can go home any time you like, you know," Minna said, hoping against hope that her cousin would decide to leave after lunch.

But Lucia had other ideas. She was looking over the field to see what she might have to work on for the summer. Meaning boys, of course. Lucia was honest about that. Apparently, Lucia was not impressed with what she had observed during the morning, for she asked Ciss whether she might accompany her to afternoon glee club practice. Ciss had been talking about the basses and how good they were in "Cradle of the Deep." Where there was a bass, there was a boy—juniors and seniors, too, instead of all these sophomores with whom she had spent the earlier part of the day.

Ciss was being gracious where Minna had been abrupt. Of course Lucia could come with her, but she would have to sit in the auditorium and be audience while the glee club performed on the stage. Ciss did not say that Lucia would have small chance of meeting boys from this location, but that was what she meant. Minna looked at her friend with admiration. How cleverly Ciss had put her cousin in her place!

Yet rumors about Minna's cousin had already spread about the school. From her striking looks, the eyes a shimmer of green beneath the iridescent shadow on the lids and from the way she dressed and acted, some thought she was a Hollywood starlet. Boys who had scarcely passed the time of day with Minna came up to greet her heartily as they left the luncheon terrace, obviously in the hope of being introduced to her guest. Minna pretended to forget what their names were, but this did not squelch them.

"They always do that when there's a new girl in town. Doesn't mean a thing," Minna said, wishing she could cut her cousin down a peg with the adroitness of Ciss.

A girl could stand only so much of this, and Minna was relieved when Lucia changed her mind again about glee club and went off with her friend. She did not, positively did not, want to give Bob Jones the opportunity to stare at her cousin all through geometry class.

Her maneuvers were in vain, however, for Bob caught up with them as they were strolling through town on the way home from school and offered them a ride in his father's shiny new car. Lucia gushed over it and over Bob, saying that she had heard so much about him. She had a beginner's license, it seemed, and she loved to drive. Though Lucia had not mentioned her license earlier, almost anyone could get one who could answer vehicle code questions; and Minna was not impressed.

Dad would never let her practice on his car, and Bob shouldn't either. She shuddered at the thought of her cousin behind the wheel of a car that, as Bob announced proudly, hadn't a scratch upon it. He had polished it this morning, and all of its Triumph Blue and its chrome gleamed from the front bumper to the back.

Lucia could hint, but she would get nowhere with Bob who had too much sense to be flattered into being reckless. Or so Minna had imagined. They had come to a quiet street with little or no traffic on it, and Lucia couldn't see any reason why a tiny try behind the wheel wouldn't be fun. She would be so very careful, and how could a girl ever learn to drive unless she had a boy to teach her?

If Bob were being nice to Lucia because she was a visiting cousin, he was certainly overdoing it. As the two of them shifted places, Minna felt very much like an unnecessary third party in the wide front seat. Lucia killed the motor immediately and had to be shown where the starter was. She moved forward with a jerk and stalled. When a car came out of a driveway, she gave a little scream and asked Bob to steer for her. Altogether, she was making Minna so nervous that she wanted to get out and walk. If she were as poor a driver as Lucia, she'd keep still about it and not play the fool. Bob must see that she was doing this only to take his whole attention. She had never known a boy to be so stupid, and she told Laura all about it that night when she called her on the phone.

"She's going to ruin my whole summer," Minna wailed from the privacy of the hall closet.

"Maybe she'll get bored with Cliffside and go away," Laura said.

"No such luck after the way she carried on at school today. She'll get a whole flock of boys to amuse her. You'll see!"

"Well, then," Laura had another suggestion, "perhaps you can turn the tables on her."

Tonight, as usual, Lucia was wakeful and wanted to chatter. She was saying it was so quiet in Cliffside that she couldn't get to sleep. Probably another of her allergies, Minna thought, burying her head in her pillow and rudely refusing to engage in further conversation. She had already heard enough about Lucia's allergies to last her for a lifetime.

Lucia couldn't wash dishes because her skin was allergic to most kinds of soap. She couldn't make her own bed because "flying particles make me sneeze." This counted her completely out of any sweeping or dusting or mopping; Minna was having to take over household tasks for the two of them.

Further, Lucia couldn't eat spinach or pork in any form—she couldn't eat so many things that Minna and her father marveled privately that she was still alive. If Lucia had been a delicate child, as Mother reminded them, it was time she outgrew it.

Not to eat what was put on your plate was a capital offense at the Vails'. Unless you were sick, Father insisted that you must. He had little patience with Lucia's insistence that eggs or pork or whatever would make her skin break out. "Nonsense," he was apt to say, beginning one of his lectures. "Who are you to be picking at your food when so many people in this world are starving to death?" If she were a homeless refugee living in a camp, she'd be lucky to have a few grains of rice. "Precious diet, my foot," he would finish. "You ought to see what it's like to go hungry."

So far as Minna could see, her cousin had allergies to anything that involved housework and family dinners, but none whatever where boys were concerned.

When Bob took the two of them out for hamburgers the following afternoon, she noticed that Lucia ate all of hers with never a qualm. She paused in her munching only to throw a bit of her roll to one of the sea gulls which circled overhead. "Dear birds," she said, acting as though she were on a mission of mercy instead of merely sitting on a flat rock near the Sea-Vue Hamburger Stand.

How could you turn the tables on a girl like this, who had so many tricks up her sleeves even when she wasn't wearing any? Today, Lucia was in a sun dress, toasting herself gently and handing Bob a bottle of tanning lotion so he could rub it on her back.

16

Bad Moments

Because moments of privacy when she could talk to Mother alone at home were rare these days, Minna sought her out in her shop. She simply could not stand her cousin, and something would have to be done about it.

"That would place your father and me in a very difficult position," Mother said soberly. "You wouldn't want that, would you?"

"N-No, but I'm in one."

"Possibly you can work out of it, dear. You can't have everything your own way in this world, you know. It wouldn't be good for you." Mother went on to explain that she felt this was the trouble with Lucia. Her parents had tried to give her the moon, and that had been a mistake; she had been coddled no end and dreadfully spoiled. Now Mother actually felt sorry for Lucia, she said. She was a restless girl who had come to the place where she didn't know *what* she wanted.

"Well, she'll want to be a Mermaid—that's obvious." Minna was out of patience even with Mother. And then she had a thought. No professional beauties or models could compete—the rules said so—and Lucia had had that bit part on television. Wouldn't that make her a professional, or something like that?

But Mother was not reassuring on this point. The film had achieved little except to go to Lucia's head. It had never been shown anywhere, but was one of those pilot projects that could not find a sponsor.

So this was the presumed Hollywood starlet who was going to the last of the Octopus parties with her and with Bob. He had included both of them in his invitation, just as though Lucia could not find her own escort. She would, when she got there, have complete choice of the stags. Minna loathed the idea of seeing Lucia sweep into the crowd and put on her airs. If Bob were so foolish as to be taken in by them, he could take Lucia, and she would stay home. She would plead a headache or toothache or whatever, but she would refuse to go. And that was that.

"Cutting off your own nose to spite your face, I'm afraid," Mother said, not pampering her on the night of the party with either hot towels or sympathy.

Minna was left to enjoy her own misery, to wonder as the hours passed what was going on at the other end of town. She got up to get a drink of water and then of milk, but she could not fall asleep. Tonight would more or less decide who the candidates for Octopus would be.

Anyone of suitable age could put his name on the list for which the people of the town could vote, but boys without backers would decide to drop out. Usually only a dozen or so of them were left by election day, and results of the contest were kept secret to heighten the excitement before the Carnival parade. Only then would the winner be revealed, as he chose his queen, and unmasked.

Also, there would be a certain amount of talk about what girls might be possible as Mermaids. Minna would be present tonight only on those few posters which Bob's artist-friend had made. Bob had loyally promised to take them along, but he could have forgotten. They were striking posters, and Minna looked just right on them. But, even if Bob had remembered, a girl on cardboard could easily be overlooked when Lucia would be attracting all the attention. Mother was right, Minna thought. She should have gone and stood up for herself.

To make matters worse—Minna was conjuring up all sorts of dreadful possibilities in her imagination—George might be at the party. He had been runner-up for Octopus last year, and he might make it this time around if he played politics with the high school crowd.

He had come back from college only yesterday, and she had helped him to unload his car. He had told her then that he would be away most of the summer. He had a job at some country club down the shore and would be leaving in the morning. But anyone knew how easy it would be for him to drive back to Cliffside tonight. The very thought shook Minna into tears.

Lucia could have Bob if he were so easy to obtain, but she couldn't have George. It wasn't as though Minna owned either of the boys, but she was prepared to fight Lucia over George. The two of them had never met, but the way this summer was going they would. Minna could feel it in her bones.

When Lucia came in finally, Minna pretended to be asleep. With all the lights turned on and Lucia humming a dance tune and whirling about, this was difficult. Minna gave up and, rolling over, said in the bored tone copied from her cousin, "Have any fun?"

"Not much, really . . . this crowd is awfully stuffy, you know, but," Lucia paused maddeningly and examined her reflection in the mirror, "I did meet the most interesting foreign boy. Divine dancer, simply divine."

So Hans Van Der Oster, too, had come under her thrall. Lucia was welcome to him. She could be the one to play Chinese Checkers for a change.

"Nobody else?" Minna hated to ask this question, but she had to know the answer.

"They're so much alike, and I can't remember all their names."

So George hadn't been there, Minna was relieved to hear. He was a boy a girl was not apt to forget.

With the beginning of vacation, Minna lolled in her bed, hoping that for once Lucia would get up ahead of her and fix breakfast. Her cousin always appeared just in time to savor the bacon Minna was frying for herself and, forgetting that pork was not on her diet, beg for a tiny piece, and a bit of the marmalade and English muffins.

It was on one of these mornings when again, despite her dainty appetite, Lucia had managed to eat half of Minna's breakfast that George Hartford rang the doorbell. His mother had run out of sugar, and could he borrow a cup or two and . . . George dropped further explanation when he glimpsed Lucia in morning-glory blue. She had floated into the hall in a garment which she called her peignoir.

"If you girls are having breakfast, I don't mean to interrupt," George said, obviously glad that he had. "That bacon smells good, Minna. How about fixing some for me?"

"I'll have a touch more, too," Lucia said, going into the dining room to entertain George while Minna slaved over a hot stove and purposely burned the bacon, hoping that the smudge of it would make them choke.

"I'd as soon settle for eggs, Minna," George called, unperturbed. He opened three windows and continued his tête-à-tête. "Where have you been keeping this cousin of yours?"

Mother was busy in another part of the house, getting ready to go to her shop, when Minna burst in upon her and pillowed her head in her lap. "It isn't fair," she sobbed. "It isn't fair at all."

When the phone rang these days, it was seldom for Minna. There were long-distance calls for her cousin—almost all from males—and there were local calls. The only boys who phoned Minna were soliciting the Octopus vote. Bob was silent, even about this, and one evening she realized why. He had been dating Lucia, and he didn't want her to know about it.

Lucia had gone out with some of her friends from the city when Bob appeared at the front door and shamefacedly inquired for her. "She—she was supposed to meet me at the movies and—and I thought maybe we missed each other or something."

"Something is right," Minna said, wanting to slam the door in his face and then thinking better of it. She and Bob had been friends for a long time, and being stood up by a girl must hurt. This was no time to gloat; one didn't leave a friend standing out there in the summer fog with a bewildered expression on his face.

"You could take me, you know," she said lightly, "except that we'd be too late for the second feature. Why don't you come on in?"

Popping corn and watching television was not a very exciting way to spend time with a boy, especially when he had another girl on his mind. All Minna could think of to talk about was skin diving, and when that subject was exhausted conversation lagged.

"You're real nice not to bawl me out, Minna, know that?" Bob made an awkward beginning at apology.

"For what?" Minna shrugged her shoulders and pretended not to understand what he meant.

"You know for what."

"Maybe I do, and maybe I don't." Minna shrugged her shoulders. "Why don't you tell me?"

"I mean—well, I mean—Lucia doesn't mean a thing to me. She was just playing me for what there was in it, I guess."

It wasn't exactly as though this were the breakup of a serious love affair, Minna thought. It had been only a short time since Lucia and Bob had met.

Again there was a silence until Bob broke it with, "You still going to back me for Octopus, Minna?"

Minna said she hadn't given it much thought lately; she had been too busy training the Grunion troupe. The final list of candidates was posted in the small frame Carnival building where the voting would take place, but she hadn't bothered to look at it. "Who's running besides you?" she asked.

When Bob named George Hartford among others, Minna made her decision. She had worked for months to get George Hartford to notice her—had fetched and toted for him—and she was still only a part of the scenery. And the very first day he had met Lucia, he had made such a fuss over her. Minna couldn't forgive him. Not ever. "Sure I'm going to vote for you, Bob. Who else?" She tried to keep the quaver out of her voice.

Because the older citizens of Cliffside claimed that the Octopus election was a "valuable education for citizenship in a democracy," even small children could vote if they could write their names. But they could vote only once. The older citizens treated the election as a solemn affair, and there would be no ballot-box stuffing in Cliffside. Groups of old ladies took turns presiding at the polls, keeping an alphabetical record of names with addresses, subjecting all comers to a stern surveillance that discouraged cheaters.

Mr. Vail was given to scoffing about the way the oldsters handled it, spending public funds on printed ballots, setting up curtained polling booths equipped with ink pads and rubber stamps. "The only difference between this and a national election is that you don't have to declare whether you're a Republican or a Democrat," he said in a loud voice to his wife and daughter who had made the mistake of accompanying him to the polls. "I suppose they'll think of that next."

"Hush, dear, look how cute they are," Mother said, pointing to several small pairs of feet in white ankle socks and black patent slippers standing on tiptoe behind the curtains of the booths. Minna could remember when she, too, had been so little she could barely reach the shelf and get hold of the rubber stamp. How thrilled she had been that very first time!

Outside, some of the boys were still electioneering from boxes set up in the street, and Ralph Roberts was among them. He had brass, and he would be there! Bob was too shy to appear in public, but Minna had expected to see George. Not that she cared, she told herself, wondering why a crowd was gathering farther down the block.

She could hear faint cries of "Hurray," and arms were raised to form an arch above a pathway that was being cleared for someone. Minna could not see who it was until, peering, she beheld Laura, under the outstretched arms of fellow townsfolk who were greeting her in this spontaneous and loving fashion. Laura in her wheelchair, running it herself, with pauses to throw kisses! It was her triumphal entry, her first public appearance since her illness. It was a moment when one thought what a lovely town Cliffside was to live in, with people so dear and so warm. Laura was coming to the polls to vote, and everyone was ecstatic—or tearful.

"I never thought I'd live to see the day." Minna's mother reached for her handkerchief, and Father's lips were quivering.

One never knew what was going to happen in Cliffside and, as father had often remarked, that was part of its charm. People were people here, and they cared. The dowagers who supervised the voting cared—the folks welcoming Laura did. Cliffside stood for something that was special, unexpected sometimes, but always there.

So many were crowding around Laura that Minna receded into the background. This was Laura's hour, and it was a wonderful one. Nothing should spoil it for Laura, and it didn't.

But for Minna the spell vanished when she saw her cousin Lucia advancing upon the arm of George Hartford and asking in a voice that was high and silly, "What's going on?"

No one bothered to go into all the details for Lucia, and George seemed embarrassed. Quite unnecessarily, he took Minna aside and explained that Lucia had almost forced him to bring her. She had been walking into town, and she had hailed him. "So what could I do?"

Apparently, he thought it a mistake to appear at the polls with any girl who might be his "first lady," and Minna agreed with him. Lucia would win him no votes for Octopus; too many other girls were already jealous of her to support George if Lucia were to be his choice. And now Minna positively would not take her cousin off George's neck, as he was requesting.

Minna was surprised at her own courage in talking back to George. She had never done it before, but a girl could be pushed just so far and no farther. "Solve your own problems," she retorted. "You're not exactly helpless, are you?"

17

A Fantastic Idea

Whatever Lucia's faults, stinginess was not one of them—Minna had to admit that. She was generous with her allowance, her cosmetics and perfumes, and also with all her clothes. "You can wear anything I have, you know," Lucia had often said. "Anything that fits."

She was repeating the offer again tonight as she rummaged through the closet in an effort to find the short evening dress she wanted to wear to the country club dance. It must be somewhere in one of the garment bags she was zipping open upon billows of chiffon and crisp organdy.

"George likes me to wear blue, you know. I guess because of that first day when we met. Remember?"

"Who could forget it?" Certainly not Minna. Morning-glory blue that could not possibly be spotted with ugly bacon grease.

"You like George, too, don't you?" Lucia detected the edge in her cousin's voice and wheeled about, her arms filled with clothes.

"Oh, so-so." Minna refused to give her cousin the satisfaction of knowing what was actually going on in her mind—how envious she was of Lucia's date.

"You're a little young for him, don't you think?"

"Aren't you?" Lucia needn't be so nasty about it, considering that she was only four months the elder.

"It's different with me. I don't care for boys my own age. They seem like children." Lucia had decided against the blue, and was trying on one frock after the other. "Most people take me for nineteen."

When Lucia finally selected the white organdy with appliques of daisies, she did look lovely in it; Minna could not help saying so. Almost any girl would be gorgeous in a frock that, worn with a white marabou cape, was fit for an angel.

After Lucia had gone, Minna ruefully decided to have her own fashion show. All of her cousin's evening wardrobe was tossed lightly over the bed and several chairs and, as Lucia had said so many times, Minna could take her choice if she wanted it. Most of the girls who entered the Mermaid contest wore formals, and Minna had none of her own. If she could find a dress here that looked as marvelous on her as the white had on Lucia, she would not have to persuade Mother to buy her one. That is, if she were to enter the contest at all. If Lucia were to win a place, and Minna were to lose, it would be altogether too much for her even to face.

Perhaps it was because her spirits were so low that none of her cousin's dresses seemed to do a thing for her. Not the whirling pink chiffon with the sequinned bodice, nor the slim blue silk sheath with the rhinestone shoulder straps, nor the wheat-colored organdy that was exactly the color of her hair. She had no sparkle in her eyes to go with the long shimmering crystal earrings that she had seen her cousin wear so effectively, nor did she care for all those bangle bracelets.

Mother, called in to look, agreed with her. Nothing of Lucia's was her style.

"Could be I don't have any," Minna said bitterly. "Lucia probably has it all, just as she gets everything else without lifting a finger."

Mother tried to console her by saying that they could look all over Cliffside tomorrow and perhaps find the perfect dress. When a girl had never worn evening clothes, it was hard to tell exactly what might suit her.

"If it were covered with diamonds, I still wouldn't like it. I—I—" Minna tried to explain, "I don't feel right in formals. They're—they're not me."

"Think of something that is, then." Mother was losing her temper. "I'm tired of your sulking, Minna, and all this feeling sorry for yourself. You've got to snap out of it."

Mother went on to say that she was lucky not to have a serious problem like Laura . . . that she should count her blessings . . . that the world wouldn't end if she never were in the Mermaid contest.

By the time she had finished her lecture, Minna was fighting mad. "I'm going to beat Lucia if it's the last thing I do," she flung over her shoulder as she stormed out of the side door of her room and into the starry night.

"A walk will do you good, dear," Mother called after her. "Why don't you run down to the store and get a quart of ice cream?"

What Minna needed was the beach, but she was forbidden to go there alone after dark. Like the early curfew that her father usually set for her and for Lucia, it was a rule that had to be obeyed. Little did Mother and Father know that Lucia made light of the curfew when it suited her, Minna thought. Several times when they were supposedly asleep, she had slipped out the side door and not returned until all hours. Much as she disliked her cousin, Minna hated to be a tattletale.

No one had ever said that Minna could not go out on a sort of promontory not far from one of the main streets; it was not isolated, and no harm could come to her there. If she could not go down to the ocean, the next best thing was to look at it, and to hear the surf as it broke against the rocks, white against the blackness of the sea. Day or night, this was one of the most beautiful spots in all of Cliffside, and Minna loved it.

As she approached, she could see that she was not to have it all to herself. The dark outlines of several people appeared in silhouette against the stars, voices loud as though with excitement. Quickening her pace, Minna, too, beheld the wonder of waters flashing with the glow of phosphorescence, as it sometimes did for several weeks during the summer when it was filled with millions of tiny organisms too minute for the eye to see. Tonight the show was an unusually spectacular one, and for many miles the ocean was alight with what Minna liked to call "fairy flotillas." It was an eerie sight, a magic one, the cold green luminosity of "witch-fire" upon every ripple, banding every wave as it arched and tumbled. Several people were walking along the shore, their footprints green and ghostly in the damp sand, and beyond were all those unearthly spangles of light.

Spangles . . . spangles . . . *spangles.* An idea had leaped into Minna's mind out of the marvels of this ocean. Her ocean, as she always chose to think of it. She could watch this display half the night, but Mother would worry about her. If she lingered much longer, she would send Father out in search.

As she swung along home with the ice cream in a paper bag, she decided not to tell even Mother about her idea for the Mermaid contest. Maybe it was a crazy one, and Mother would discourage her. She could make what she needed herself or, even better, borrow it from Laura who had been a majorette in the high school drum corps. She could practice up at Laura's, too, and only Laura would be in on the secret.

As she ate her share of the chocolate ice cream which she had purchased because it was the family's favorite, she could have been spooning oatmeal for all the attention that she gave to it. With a quart there would be a round of seconds, but Dad could have hers. She had other things to think about, things far more important than chocolate ice cream.

"You aren't sick, are you, Minna?" Mother asked, astonished at her strange loss of appetite.

"No, I feel real good. Lots and lots better than when I went out."

Minna's mind was spinning with a thousand details. The contest was close—not many days away—and she would have to work fast. Hans Van Der Oster would have to help her, but she would tell him only part of what she had in mind. She would call him first thing in the morning, she decided, and ask him to give her special dancing lessons. Thank heavens, he was still in town and would not leave for Holland until the end of summer school.

Bob had said he would back her to the limit, and she would ask him to give instructions to the orchestra when the big night came. Hans would tell her what number they should play when her turn came to appear on the stage. Unless her courage failed her at the very last moment, she was going to make Cliffside sit up and take notice of Minnow Vail.

Later, when she tried to get to sleep, she could not. Again and again she was picturing the whole scene so vividly that she could hear the audience clapping. Or would they laugh at her instead? It was a chance she had to take.

"I told you not to wait up for me," Lucia said when finally she appeared and found Minna reading a book. Glancing at the clock, Minna saw that it was almost four in the morning. Mother would be furious at George for keeping her out this late, and Minna mentioned it.

"Oh, George? I lost him early in the evening. I met a boy I knew from Beverly Hills and. . . ." Lucia was fumbling with the zipper of her rumpled dress. "Help me out of this, will you? I'm simply dead."

"You look it," Minna said harshly. "You look like something the cat dragged in and didn't like." Lucia's lipstick had vanished along with one of her earrings, and so had her carefully arranged coiffure. She had altogether the appearance of a girl who had been necking for hours in the back seat of some car, and it was not a particularly pretty sight.

How any girl could walk out on a dream date such as the one with George was more than Minna could imagine. Minna had the feeling that he would make her suffer for it somehow. Maybe you could stand up a boy like Bob and get away with it, but you couldn't do that to George Hartford.

Though she had slept so sketchily, Minna was up early to begin to put her plan in operation. She was so stimulated that she was not even tired when she called Hans and said mysteriously that she was about to ask a special favor of him. Since he lived up in the hills near Laura's, it wouldn't be too much trouble for him to run over there, would it? He went to summer school in the mornings, Minna knew, but afternoon would be fine. Laura's house wouldn't be hard for him to find and . . . .

"Whatever are you up to, Minna?" Mother came into the hall just as Minna was finishing her guarded conversation.

"You'll see, Mom, you'll see." Minna ran out to the shower room at the back of the house where she always dressed for the beach, and made up a bulky package. It would be too heavy for her to carry if she had to walk up to Laura's, but nothing daunted her this morning.

She had glimpsed George out washing his car and, if she helped him, she might be able to persuade him to drive her up there before he took off for the country club where he was giving golf lessons.

"Your cousin get back all right last night?" George asked in a grim tone, his ears turning a bright shade of red. He was still flustered and angry, but Minna was not going to make it easy for him.

"You took her, didn't you? You should know."

For answer, she got only a growl as George handed her the chamois skin and asked her to dry off the upper part of the car while he hosed the wheels. "I'll do a good job only if you'll drive me up to Laura's afterwards," Minna said, naming a price for her services that, earlier, had always been free.

"Women, they're all alike." George was temperamental, and Minna had never seen him in a nastier mood. It boded ill for her cousin. One of these days, Lucia would get her comeuppance.

"I'll be up at the Adamses' if you want me for anything," Minna called to her mother as she came down to get her awkward bundle and stow it in George's car. The Adamses would ask her to stay to lunch, she knew. They always did, wanted her to spend as much time as she could with Laura. This was not the day for Laura's therapy, and her friend was sure to be at home. She hadn't called Laura because she wanted to surprise her.

The way she was arranging her plan, it would all have to be worked out up at Laura's. Every time the two girls got together, Laura had been urging her to go into the Mermaid contest. She'd have to do it this year for both of them, and this would be Laura's opportunity to get in on some of the excitement.

"Whatever have you got in there?" George took the package from her and eyed it curiously. "Must be rocks from the weight of it."

"Right, George, it's rocks. I'm making an anchor, didn't you know?"

"Fine day to be so cheerful." George glowered at her and looked at his watch. "I'm going to be late if I take you up there. Ever think of that?"

"A bargain's a bargain." Minna settled herself firmly in the front seat. "Drive on."

"You've changed a lot, do you know that, Minna?"

"For the better, I hope." Was George at last about to give her a compliment?

"Could be." If George were about to say more, he apparently thought better of it, and he lapsed into silence.

When George dropped her off at the Adamses' and she thanked him, she heard him say astoundingly, "My pleasure." Was he only saying it to be polite after his gruffness, or did it mean something? Sometimes she thought she would never understand boys.

She would have to ask Laura what she thought about it. There was so much to talk about with Laura that she wouldn't know where to begin.

"You girls have been giggling for over an hour," Mrs. Adams said, coming finally to the closed door of Laura's room where the two of them were buzzing like bees. "Whatever is so funny?" She rattled the knob, about to come in and investigate.

"Wait a minute, Mom, will you?"

Hastily, Minna kicked her package under the bed. She liked Mrs. Adams and knew that she could trust her but, until Hans came, could not be sure that the most important part of her idea was feasible.

"Of course, I know where your majorette costume is," Mrs. Adams said in answer to her daughter's question, "but whatever for?"

"Minna wants to borrow part of it—something to do with the Carnival." Again Laura burst into a gale of giggles in which Minna joined her.

"I never saw such girls," Mrs. Adams said, but not unkindly. Anything that would make Laura laugh was good for her.

If Minna were to be here for several hours, she would go into town, Mrs. Adams said. Now with Billy away at summer camp, she had been rather tied down and she needed to go to the beauty parlor.

"You can stay all afternoon, if you like," Minna said, trying not to sound too enthusiastic. She and Hans, with Laura, could have the whole big living room to themselves. The Adamses had an extensive collection of records, and Hans would be sure to find several that were suitable. They could kick back the rug and there would be loads of room in which to practice.

"That's awfully nice of you, Minna. I can't tell you how much I appreciate it." Mrs. Adams beamed on her in a way that made Minna feel a bit like a hypocrite. There was plenty for lunch in the refrigerator, and lots of lemonade and cookies. What luck, Minna thought. Hans was always agreeable when you stuffed him with cookies, and she was going to have to ask a lot of him.

Almost too much, perhaps. She could see by the expression on his face when he came that he thought her request was absurd. Possibly he could teach her to do a soft-shoe routine in a few days' time, but even he could not do one handicapped by heavy objects on his feet, such as she was suggesting. It was impossible, he said, forgetting his English then and lapsing into a stream of Dutch that could have been swearing.

"A person never knows until they try, do they?" Minna turned on the stereo with a catchy record on it. "You're the best dancer in town, Hans. Do you know that? All the girls are saying so."

If she could not weaken Hans with cookies, she would

do it with compliments. "Come on, Hans, you show me. I told Laura you could do it, and you don't want to disappoint her, do you? When she's heard all these wonderful things. . . ?"

18

"We Want Minnow!"

Whatever Minna was plotting, Mother was happy to see that she had stopped drooping and was cheerful. Dad was calling her "Miss Mystification," and Minna would have taken both of them into her confidence except for Lucia's inquisitiveness. A chance word might give her cousin a clue, and Lucia was in a dither to discover why she was going up to Laura's house each day.

"Can't I come with you?" Lucia was asking. "It's lonesome staying here by myself with no one at home but the cat."

She could call some boy and ask him to take her to the beach. Certainly Lucia had not run out of boys, had she? Minna was making it clear that, at the moment, Lucia could pick up her own loose ends. Minna was too busy to bother either with her or her questions as to whether she was intending to drop out of the Mermaid contest. If Minna were still going to be in it, whatever was she going to wear?

Lucia had determined upon the pink chiffon for herself, but Minna could have the yellow organdy or any of her others. If Minna had found another dress in one of the shops, what color was it, and why on earth couldn't she see it?

"I declare, you've closed up like a clam," Lucia said when another of her attempts at prying had failed. "I never saw the like of it."

"Wait until I open up."

"I don't see there's much to jig about," Lucia pouted as Minna danced across to the door and departed, carrying a bag of cookies for Hans. He was coming over to the Adamses' again to help her practice and give her pointers on how to handle herself. He had guessed most—but not all—of her secret, but he had promised not to breathe a word of it to anyone.

Minna did not register for the contest until the last open day, and her cousin was further tantalized when she made no beauty parlor appointment to have her hair done on either the morning or the afternoon of the Big Night.

"You're not going with your hair looking like it usually does, are you?" Lucia said when Minna was making no preparations except to wash it and twist a few curls around her face with bobby pins.

"I'll finish it off with your lacquer later, if you don't mind," Minna said, wishing her cousin would stop pestering her with offers of this, that, and the other thing. Earrings? Bracelets? A necklace? Clear plastic slippers? "No, thanks, I have everything I need up at the Adamses'."

Minna was checking through her arrangements to be sure that she had covered everything that she possibly could foresee. Hans was to give her a last rehearsal. Bob would cue the orchestra and get his crowd of boys to clap when he saw her standing in the wings. Mr. Adams would drive her, and she would put on her outfit in one of the auditorium dressing rooms below the stage.

"It's every girl for herself tonight, Dad, don't you think?" Minna said, stroking her father's cheek affectionately so that he would not be hurt because she was not going with him and Lucia and Mother. "You'll see what I mean later when the curtain goes up. Honestly, you will."

All she needed from Lucia now was one of her green sticks of iridescent eye shadow, a box of mascara, and an eyebrow pencil, please. Mr. Adams was going to make her up, she said. He had lots of little theater experience and knew the ropes.

She rushed out the door and returned as quickly because she had forgotten the most important things of all—bear hugs for her mother and her father. "Wish me luck, will you?"

Minna was calm all through her supper at the Adamses'. Thoughtfully, Mrs. Adams had prepared something light—poached eggs on toast—before what she called Minna's Big Performance. She felt steady all the while Mr. Adams was applying the make-up to give her the appearance of "someone out of this world." It was not until Laura changed her mind about going along to watch the contest that Minna began to have the first twinges of stage fright.

"If I were there to see you lose, I'd cry my eyes out." Laura excused herself. "I'd rather wait home and have you come up and tell me all about it afterwards."

By the time Minna reached the big old auditorium with Mr. Adams and saw the crowds already milling about in front of it, she was ready to flee in a panic. "Steady now, there, girl," Mr. Adams said. "Take good deep breaths—don't hurry—and you'll do fine."

Minna did not agree—she was going to be a flop, and she knew it. The crowd would not applaud, and some might boo. The judges would be swayed by audience reaction, and she would be lucky if she were not eliminated in the first round. She just knew she would never reach the finals.

She was conscious only of a general blur of faces as she brushed through a mass of taffeta and tulle to reach the back entrance to the auditorium, only to find her way blocked by a man at the door who was checking in all the contestants and giving them numbers to indicate the order of their appearances. Fortunately, the line was still a scattered one. Most of the other girls were still chattering to their respective throngs of devotees, but those within earshot tittered when Minna, carrying her large package, but wearing only a simple cotton dress, was told to go around to the front. "This is for contestants only," the man said firmly. "All others use the main entrance."

"But I am a contestant," Minna insisted, giving her name. "I'm on the list."

Mr. Adams had suggested that she go to the farthest dressing room because it was little used, and this early in the evening she had it all to herself. From his little theater days, Mr. Adams was thoroughly familiar with the old auditorium and its workings, and he pointed out that this dressing room had a further advantage. Because of the way sound carried to it, one could hear exactly what was transpiring directly above upon the stage. It was here that he had waited for his own cues.

She should have used more of her cousin's lacquer, Minna thought, brushing out her blond locks but wishing they were stiffer, and more like a wig. As she yanked and pulled her way into the rest of her outfit, she was remembering her conversation with her mother on the night when she was trying on all of her cousin's formals and hadn't liked them. Mother had suggested that she try something that was truly hers, and that was exactly what she was doing tonight. "If this isn't me, there isn't any me."

It was eerie to be alone in this shadowy dressing room tapping her feet to the orchestra which had begun its overture. In her mind's eye, she could see her mother and her father settling into their seats, fanning themselves with their programs, nervously chatting. She could hear the master of ceremonies announcing the first number, by an aging soprano once famous at the Metropolitan Opera in New York. Cliffside was loaded with talent—much of it from other years, but all eager to perform on state occasions. The soprano was followed by a tenor and then by a pianist, all of whom responded generously with encores.

Finally, it was time for Minna to begin edging her way out of the dressing room. She could not walk swiftly, and getting up the stairs would be best if she did it backwards. She used this technique in the ocean to keep the waves from knocking her down. Tonight there were other types of waves, waves of laughter from the other contestants, as she slipped into the twenty-first place. Maybe Bob wouldn't recognize her in her present getup—maybe he had forgotten to cue the orchestra to the number she would need when it was her turn to cross the stage.

So many girls were competing that the line stretched clear outside, with Minna slightly past the middle of it. There must be at least fifty girls, some wearing ball gowns, and all but one in some type of formal.

Lucia was far to the front, preoccupied with last touches of make-up. Apparently she had given up looking around for her cousin, for her eyes were fixed upon the stage where the first girl in line was starting a solitary promenade that was painful. She walked with a slouch and met with only a spatter of applause. From what Minna could hear of it, back where she stood, it must be only from her relatives.

Other girls fared somewhat better, but audience reaction was spotty until Lucia, moving with graceful poise, won a hearty response that, unless all signs failed, would put her in the finals. Minna's heart sank, and she lost count then of who did—and who didn't—meet with favor.

She was moving forward steadily until she was standing just to one side of the curtain where Bob could see her if he were on the alert. She had given her number and her name, and now the voice over the loud speaker was booming, "Number twenty-one . . . Minna Vail. Take her away."

Good old Bob! He had told the orchestra, and they were shifting into her number—"Darktown Strutter's Ball."

Now, if Cliffside wanted a Mermaid, it could have her modern style. A girl dressed in a black skin diving suit, wearing a borrowed spangled cape, and doing a soft-shoe dance with her great frog flippers. De-dah-de-DAH! de-dah-de-DAH! de-dah-dah-dum-dum-DAH!

Later Hans told her that she had missed a beat or two, and had not gotten back to the timing as quickly as she should have after one of her cart wheels. The truth of the matter was, as Minna explained, that she could scarcely hear the music above the crowd's roar.

Bob said he had started the stomping, and her father reported that he had been first to shout, "We want Minnow." But, whatever the original source, others had been quick to follow; and Minna had, as the saying goes, "brought down the house."

Reviewing her great moment of triumph afterward, Minna told Laura she could not quite remember all that happened next. She was in such a daze that it seemed to her it must be some other girl who was taking her place among the finalists. As the spotlight played upon each of them in turn, people in the audience stood up and chanted, "We want Minnow . . . we want Minnow," until, in order to silence them, the master of ceremonies asked her to repeat her first performance. Again, the crowd went wild.

Then she was being led over to the judges' box to receive congratulations. She had placed first beyond a doubt—first of the Mermaids to be chosen. Standing aside with a big bouquet of red roses tied with the blue prize ribbon to watch the selection of the nine other Mermaids, she faced the blinding light of news photographers' flash bulbs.

She was hazy about the rest of it—whether Lucia had placed fifth or sixth—about the names of people who crowded to the footlights when the show was over to greet her and wish her well. It was so hot here, so desperately hot in this skin-tight rubber suit. Would nobody open a window? Would nobody give her a breath of air?

Dad said later that he had seen her swaying and her face grow white. He had pushed his way to the front and caught her in his arms. The next thing she knew she was being doused with a pitcher of ice water, and she was sitting up and spluttering. "Can't hurt my outfit anyway, can it?" she remembered herself saying to her father as she managed a twisted grin.

There was to be no more excitement for Minna Vail tonight. Mother and Father were firm about that until Minna mentioned Laura. She had been sitting up there and waiting, and she would be crushed if they didn't stop by. It wasn't as though they had to bother about Lucia . . . take her home and all. Lucia had vanished, presumably in a pet, without a word to any of the Vails—to return as it suited her. And the Adamses had been so grand about everything. . . .

"You win again," Father said, packing all her paraphernalia in the back seat of the car, except for the roses. "Quit tickling my nose, will you?"

Minna was dividing her flowers so that Laura could have half of them. If things had been different, Laura would have been there with her. Laura had said that Minna must compete for both of them, and she was entitled to her share of the first-prize bouquet. "Don't you see how it is, Mom?"

"Of course, dear, anything you can do for Laura. . . ."

The Adamses had already heard the news from neighbors, and all three of them were ecstatic. They were rejoicing in Minna's big evening, and Laura was saying that next year she would give Minna a run for her money when she burst into hysterical, uncontrollable sobs that were pitiful for everyone to hear.

"Our girls can't stand too much excitement," both sets of parents agreed as they bade each other a warm and understanding good night.

19

How You Feel Inside

"It was because Laura hadn't had any fun for so long. That's why she cried," Minna said as the three Vails sat around the Sunday breakfast table, leisurely discussing the events of the previous evening. Lucia had come in late, and was still asleep. "I don't think she was jealous of me, like I was of her before she got sick."

"Yes, it's too bad Laura has had to miss out on so much," Mother agreed, "but wonderful that she is so much stronger. Her mother was saying last night that she really could get out a great deal more than she does. The doctors say that it would be good for her to mingle. . . ."

When the phone started ringing, Father didn't want anyone to answer it. He had more claim on Minna than her public did, he said, and he didn't know whether he could stand living in the same house with a celebrity. As the phone continued its shrill summons, he suggested taking the day away for a picnic, a whimsey that met no support whatever from Mother. With all the tourists in town, Sunday was her best day at the gift shop, and she could not afford to lose the business.

"Well, I'm going fishing then," he said, half-jokingly, shoving his chair away from the table and departing with half his breakfast uneaten. "If anyone wants me, I'll be down at Joe's Coffee Shop."

"Where he will do nothing but boast about you," Mother said with a smile, "the way he did last night. To everyone within earshot."

As the morning went on, Minna had so many calls that her answers became almost mechanical. She was thrilled to death . . . imagine it happening to her . . . she had never expected . . . and so forth and so on. It was exhilarating to be borne on such a tide of well-wishers, and to have an appointment to be fitted into one of the long, slinky, silvery sheaths that was always a Mermaid costume. Bob was insisting that she save all the dances for him at Neptune's Ball, and she had agreed to give him half of them. "But suppose you turn out to be the Octopus?" she had teased him. "Then who are you going to ask?"

Her Grunion days were over, all this frolicking through the parade and along the line of march. Now, as a Mermaid, she would ride on one of the two major floats surrounding the throne of Neptune or his queen Amphitrite. And later, she would be again on the stage of the auditorium as part of the glittering pageant that opened Neptune's Ball. After her astounding victory, the rest would be easy as sitting down.

Minna was sprawling now on the floor of the hall, an unglamorous but comfortable position from which to continue her endless telephone conversations. It seemed to her that everyone in town had called except Laura. As the day wore on, Laura became uppermost in Minna's mind. Should she call Laura, or shouldn't she, and if she did what would she say? Mere words couldn't bridge the sad gulf that lay between a girl who could dance and walk and one who couldn't.

The important thing to Minna was that she had won a victory that proved something to herself and to her world. Minna had made her point; she could be a Mermaid if she chose to be. And, now that she had won, what next? It was like swimming out to the farthermost rock and asking herself where do we go from here? Her line of thought was getting so complicated and confusing that Minna decided to abandon it altogether and go down to the beach.

With all her practicing up at the Adamses', she had not been swimming for ages—a number of days, anyway. It would be a relief now not to have to figure anything out, not to answer any more phone calls, but merely to plunge into the surf. She would not go to any of the main beaches where droves of people likely would come and congratulate her. She wanted to be by herself in a cove that few frequented because it was hard to reach, the cove where she and Bob had gone skin diving the day she encountered the eel. Skin divers might be there, but skin divers were usually the taciturn type of folk who could take Mermaids or leave them alone.

The waves were gentle today—gentle and clear as panes of glass reflecting patterns of brown and orange and purple seaweed. The ocean was in no hurry today; neither was Minna, swimming leisurely or pausing to rest upon kelp-covered rocks. The sea surged easily around her, coming and going and coming; while beneath the surface, like flashes of sunlight, she could see the schools of tiny fish, most of them baby grunions, or so she had been told.

So the Grunion troupe ashore no longer had its leader, all those babies—some as young as six—whom she had been training. There were so many of the young Grunions crowding into the grade school gymnasium where she had been teaching them to do cart wheels and handsprings that she had quite lost track of their ages which must be anywhere from six to fourteen or fifteen. Their mothers were supposed to supply their costumes, and for weeks the local yardgoods store had been out of gold and silver metallic cloth. Frantic parents were sending to the city so that their darling boys and girls might be properly arrayed for their various antics.

This year the Grunions would be running mischievously about while Minna viewed them from her float and did nothing but wave to the crowd and smile. Her Grunions—Minna was suddenly sentimental about them and all the good times.

Somehow the ocean, as always, made thoughts pop into her head that would not have been there otherwise. Why could not Laura take her place on the float and even afterward at the pageant? With her white skin and her raven hair, she was as pretty a girl as any that had passed before the judges, and Minna had long wanted to make it up to Laura. She had been so nasty to her in the last few days before her dreadful illness that it had haunted her. She had wanted to make it better for Laura, and this could be the way.

"It's the nicest thing I ever heard of a girl wanting to do." Surprisingly, Lucia was the first to give voice when Minna opened the whole subject at dinner that night.

"It's not that I'm noble, or anything." Minna wanted to make her point of view clear to herself as well as to the others at the table. "It's just that—well—it would make me feel awfully good inside."

She explained further that being a Grunion wouldn't bother her a bit when she didn't have to . . . when she had another choice. And that was, perhaps the whole of it; but Father thought differently.

"Do unto others," he said, and added with a lighter touch, "before they do you."

"Will you please stop looking at me so hard, all of you?" Minna cried, flushing with embarrassment.

The whole town would hear about Minna's decision, but this was inevitable when it was keyed up to Carnival pitch. Everyone knew that the Adamses had checked with the doctor, and the doctor had said he thought Laura could stand whatever strain might be involved. Everyone had heard that two of the judges had agreed to Minna's request, but the third had opposed it and had been overruled. The whole proceeding was highly irregular, some said, agreeing with the third judge, and might start a dangerous precedent. Others said nothing like this had ever happened before, and likely wouldn't again. And so it went. Cliffside was serious about everything connected with its Carnival.

Months of preparation were reaching their climax, and some even claimed to know who had been elected Octopus. Whispers went around, naming several different boys and leaving the choice still a matter of rumor.

Merchants were putting the finishing touches on their shop decorations for Carnival week; windows were bursting with Davy Jones Lockers, treasure chests, ship models, fish in wild colors, and all manner of gay and imaginative displays. Women were wearing fantastic beach hats and gobs of shell jewelry; men went about their business in sport shirts gaudily printed with marine designs. During Carnival week, anyone caught without some sign of the sea about his person must pay a forfeit. To enforce this Order of Neptune, a raffish crew of "Beachcombers" roamed the streets in search of unfortunate souls who defied this august ruling and made them sing sea chanteys, climb rope ladders, or some such nonsense.

However sedate it might be at other seasons of the year, Cliffside played with wild abandon at Carnival time.

Conservative citizens dressed as sailors and danced the hornpipe; artists emerged from their studios arrayed as sea nymphs and mermen.

Hundreds of visitors were streaming into town, and by the morning of the parade traffic was bumper to bumper. It had taken all night to assemble some of the elaborate homemade floats that now began to creak into position, with Grunions leaping on and off them and getting in everyone's way, as was to be expected of Grunions. They were the imps of the parade, assigned to the job of making mischief and selling souvenirs.

When the corps of motorcycle police opened the event with a scream of sirens and an exhibition of maneuvers, it was Grunions who jumped upon the handle bars. Grunions ran about snatching batons mid-air from drum majorettes, throwing them off stride and out of patience. Grunions did a hysterical hula in imitation of the Hawaiian dancers—improvisations were the order of the Grunion day.

As the leader of the Grunion troupe, Minna darted ceaselessly here and there, pausing only to check on whether Laura had arrived to take her place upon the float with Neptune; whether everything was all right with Laura in the Court of the Mermaids. Every year Neptune's float grew more beautiful, people said, and now its decorators had quite outdone themselves with crystal and tinted coral trees and arrangements of great white shells in which the Mermaids sat. Laura's face was so glowing that she was quite the loveliest of all.

The parade moved on and on, as such parades did. One of the druggists had a float that depicted Neptune taking tranquilizers and a sign that read CALM YOURSELF. A department store showed fish doing their Christmas shopping early and remarking, "It's better when you buy it in Cliffside." Which was rushing things a bit, onlookers murmured, when it was barely past the Fourth of July. "If you have any trouble with sea serpents, call us," the local exterminator urged, depicting a horrendous dragonlike creature. And so it went, sometimes with long pauses when some float stalled or broke down altogether and had to be hauled ignominiously away. Grunions filled in the gaps with exhibitions of handsprings and cart wheels, or seized this chance to vend their shell souvenirs.

When the Octopus arrived, accompanied by drummers and a fanfare of trumpets, every girl's heart quickened its beat. Somewhere, sometime along the line of march, he would make his choice from among them and name his queen. It was impossible for Minna to guess who this hooded form might actually be, whose face was concealed behind the grotesque mask with its leering yellow eyes. Six long black arms waved snakily from a rotund black frame suspended from his shoulders. His own two arms were gloved, and with them he was playing ring-around-rosy with a six-year-old Grunion who was trying desperately to escape from the monster.

Singling out various maiden ladies of uncertain age but outlandish costume, he embraced each in turn while onlookers cheered. The Octopus was having a ball, and so was the crowd, many of whom had arrived before dawn to take over the choicest locations. Meanwhile, various Grunions had found a large paper whale abandoned by less active souls and were running about in it with an enthusiasm undiminished either by the hot sun or the weary blocks they had already traveled.

Still to be seen were the Mermaids surrounding Neptune and Amphitrite. According to reports which Minna had from her various adjutants, Neptune's float had been blocked by one of the street barricades, and Amphitrite's vehicle had a flat tire. Whatever the cause of these delays to the long parade's climax, Minna rather welcomed them. She had had a hectic day thus far—though it had been fun, and she did not now relish seeing Lucia reclining gracefully and throwing kisses.

Nevertheless, the Octopus had vanished from her view. According to several of the all-seeing, all-knowing Grunions, he was heading toward the other end of town. Minna was all too aware that this was where the Mermaids were assembled. The information made her uneasy, and she was not further reassured by the distant sound of drums beating a rat-tat-tat that was rising to crescendo.

"Use a bicycle if you have to," she ordered one of her loyal aides, "but get up there as fast as you can, and come back faster."

As the youngster returned and skidded to a stop, he had the look of a bearer of important tidings. "Seems like the Octopus is picking his girl," he panted. "It's as good as done. Everybody says so. And I saw it myself. He had one of the Mermaids sitting on his lap, and all."

"Which one of them was it?" Minna took the bicycle from him with hands that trembled.

"How should I know?" The youngster drew a stick of bubble gum from his pocket and prepared to chew it. "Lots of pretty girls up there, but no prettier than you."

Minna could tell by his awkward compliment, so unlike him, that he was concealing something from her. "You tell me, or you'll be sorry."

"It isn't me that will be sorry, Minnow. It's you. It was your cousin."

So it was all over, and everything had been decided. Everything had fallen into Lucia's silken lap like ripe figs from a tree which she had not even had to shake. It was like that with some people, but Minna was not one of their number.

Seeking a secret refuge in which to hide with her bitter disappointment, Minna could find only a filling station's powder room. Powder rooms were always a girl's last resort, and she would stay here tearing paper towels from the roll and tossing them crumpled into the basket until all of Cliffside went home to soak its parade-weary feet. She would stay here until, well, she got thirsty. Thought of the Coke machine outside with its ice-cold drinks was a tempting one.

"Wherever have you been? I've been looking all over. . . ."

Dime in hand, Minna turned at the sound of a voice

muffled by a hood and a mask. She was facing the Octopus, and the voice was adding, "Don't you know me?"

"How would I?" Minna could do no more than whisper. "You could be anyone."

"Anyone?" The Octopus tossed off his hood, showing a crew cut soaked with perspiration so that she could not determine the color of his hair. The crew cut could belong to Ralph Roberts, to Bob Jones, or. . . . "Guess," the voice still behind the lurid mask insisted.

"I couldn't, possibly." Minna held on to one of the gasoline pumps, hoping that it would sustain her equilibrium, and wishing there were not so many Grunions suddenly crowding around her. This should be a girl's private moment, if she were ever to have one.

"Let's get rid of these twerps, shall we?" As the Octopus removed his mask, she beheld the audacious, grinning face of none other than George Hartford. "Still mad at me, Minnow?"

"Wh-why. . . ." Minna was utterly confused. George Hartford obviously was about to ask her to be his queen, and her mind should have been shooting off Roman candles. And yet it wasn't. Even a few weeks earlier, this would have been the most thrilling moment of her life. George Hartford, so long the boy of her dreams, was choosing her above all other girls. After ignoring her as a person with feelings, never asking her for a date, never helping her as Bob had done! He had never seen her as anyone except "the little kid across the street," and *now he must be choosing her only to humiliate Lucia.* George and Lucia were two-of-a-kind, as her father would say. It was all suddenly clear to Minna.

Scenes were running through her mind as though she were at the movies, while the eagerly watching Grunions anticipated a final clinch. She could not embarrass George by refusing to be his queen, refusing to come into the embrace of six serpentine arms and two of his own.

"Kings and queens often play games, don't they?" Minna murmured, turning her face so that his lips only brushed against her cheek.

Bob would never call her again, never think that he had a chance. She had lost Bob forever, and Bob was real. He was the boy she cared about—she knew that now. Plain old Bob Jones . . .

Bob, who worked part time in her father's hardware store, which would be open tonight because of all the tourists in town. "Hi, Bob," she said, sidling in hours after the parade was over and making a special point of her greeting.

"Hello yourself, Queen." Bob was brusque and businesslike, excusing himself to sell fishing rods.

Waiting for him beside the cash register, Minna whispered, "I'm still saving half of my dances at the Ball for you, and—and I wish you could have all of them."

"You mean that?" Bob fumbled with change for the customers and forgot to add the state sales tax. Father would have a fit when he came back from supper-leave.

"Yes, I do."

One could scarcely say that an array of lawn rakes

made a romantic arbor or a shield from prying eyes, and yet that was the way it was. When you kissed for the first important time, Minna thought, it did not matter where you were. Only how you felt inside, clear down to the tips of your toes.

WHITMAN BOOKS FOR GIRLS